KT-476-932

Dover Beats
the Band

The
Chief Inspector Wilfred Dover
Novels

Dover One
Dover Two
Dover Three
It's Murder With Dover
Dover and the Unkindest Cut of All
Dover Beats the Band
Dover Goes to Pott
Dover and the Claret Tappers
Dover Strikes Again
Dead Easy for Dover

Dover Beats the Band

A Detective Chief Inspector
Wilfred Dover Novel

By Joyce Porter

A Foul Play Press Book

The Countryman Press, Inc.
Woodstock, Vermont

For Donna Bradbrooke,
with kindest regards

One

'And I'll tell you something else for free,' growled Detective Chief Inspector Dover, speaking straight from his stomach. 'I can do without looking at nasty messes like this right after my bloody lunch!'

The small group of men, gum-booted and with their coat collars turned up against the biting wind, exchanged glances. They could hardly quarrel with the sentiment expressed; it was just that it sounded rather odd coming from the lips of a member of Scotland Yard's Murder Squad.

'It is a bit unpleasant, sir,' agreed Inspector Telford after a pause.

'Unpleasant?' sneered Dover through the grubby hand-kerchief he had clamped over his mouth and nose. 'It's bloody horrible! I could throw up right now without thinking twice about it.'

'Well, if you've seen all you want to, sir, we might as well go over to the Operations Room we've set up in that caravan over there . . .'

Detective Chief Inspector Dover was already under way. Although a man of considerable – not to say excessive – bulk, he was extremely nippy where his own personal convenience and comfort were concerned. He plunged ahead now, slipping and stumbling across the unsavoury expanse of Muncaster's municipal rubbish dump, parts of which were still smoking obscenely in the icy drizzle. Inspector Telford strode along more athletically in the rear. He was the representative of the local police force who had been detailed to act as liaison officer to the two bigwigs who'd come down from London to take over the investigation. Inspector Telford had already spent several hours on and around the huge rubbish dump – ever since the two labourers from the Sanitary Department had first reported finding the body, in fact – and he wasn't at all sorry to be getting away from the stink himself for a bit.

The third member of this little retreating group was Detective Sergeant MacGregor, Chief Inspector Dover's assistant, dog's-body and general whipping boy. Being a conscientious police officer as well as a handsome and personable young man, he was the only one who regretted having to leave the scene of the crime. The naked body of the dead man with its blackened and disfigured head and shoulders was not a pretty sight, but it warranted more than the cursory glare it had got from Dover. Without a doubt, murder had been committed and it was the duty of every detective to knuckle down and bring the perpetrator to justice. Still, for the time being MacGregor had no choice but to follow his lord and master so he salved his conscience by bestowing an encouraging smile on the bunch of uniformed constables who were left poking sullenly around in the steaming rubbish for clues.

As they approached the edge of the dump, which was luckily not more than a dozen or so yards away, Inspector Telford put a spurt on and caught Dover up.

'This is where they must have broken through, sir,' he said helpfully, indicating a stretch of the barbed-wire fencing which had been carefully roped off. 'They cut the wire there, you see, and then, when they left, they must have carefully stretched it back into place. From a distance you wouldn't really notice it had been cut. It was only because they started working down at this end of the dump this morning that the workmen spotted the damage and began . . .'

But Dover wasn't lending more than a quarter of an ear. He had got the large caravan in which the local police had established their mobile Serious Incidents Room firmly in his sights and was surging relentlessly towards it. Not until he was safely inside, ensconced in the most comfortable chair available and with a lavish supply of tea and cakes in front of him, would anything be able to wrench his butterfly mind back to the grim business in hand.

Eventually Inspector Telford took up his tale again. In spite of some pretty strong evidence to the contrary, he still couldn't quite bring himself to believe that Dover simply didn't want to know. A senior Scotland Yard detective not interested in the mysterious discovery of a dead body? It wasn't possible . . . was it? 'We made a preliminary examination as best we could, sir, without disturbing the body. Of course, we'll know more of what we're up against when we get the post morten results and the various lab reports. Meanwhile, we've got a few basic facts to go on. The dead body is that of a man . . .'

'Any fool could see that!' sniggered Dover through a mouthful of chocolate éclair.

'The body is completely naked, sir,' Inspector Elford continued stiffly. 'As far as we have been able to ascertain all the clothing has been removed and there is no sign of any personal possessions whatsoever. We haven't been able to search underneath the body as yet, but I doubt if we'll find anything. Whoever deposited chummy out there didn't intend him to be indentified easily, even if he was found. The damage inflicted on the head and shoulders proves that.'

Sergeant MacGregor was busy taking notes. Of course, he and Dover should have been out there, in the field, discovering all this for themselves. It was galling to have to rely upon the half-baked theories of this country bumpkin. 'What was the cause of death?'

'I was just coming to that, sergeant.' Inspector Telford wasn't over-enamoured at being barked at by prissy young sergeants from London. 'It looks as though he was strangled. Judging by the marks round his neck, he was garotted by a cord or a thin rope.'

'There's nothing still tied round the neck?'

'No. Whatever it was has been removed.'

MacGregor turned to a fresh page in his notebook. 'And this damage to the head and shoulders, sir?' he prompted.

'It looks as though he's been burnt. Nothing very deep. Just enough to singe off the hair and blacken the skin. What it adds up to, of course, is that we're not going to be able to produce a recognisable photograph of the dead man for identification purposes.'

'Have you any idea yet what caused it?'

Inspector Telford shrugged his shoulders. 'Not at the moment. I'd guess something like petrol or paraffin poured over his head and set alight.'

'After death, do you think?'

Inspector Telford grimaced. 'Jesus, I hope so!'

'They might have used acid,' said MacGregor thoughtfully.

'How about a blowlamp?' Dover made his contribution with much hilarity as he reached across to forcibly abduct the last cake. 'A blowlamp'd give anybody a short-back-and-sides, eh?'

The arrival of a despatch rider with a large envelope spared Inspector Telford the embarrassment of finding a rejoinder to this grisly suggestion. The envelope contained the photographs which had been taken earlier of the dead man as he lay on his side in his shallow grave amongst the rubbish.

MacGregor studied the photographs as Inspector Telford passed them across. 'There wasn't much of an effort made at concealment,' he said accusingly. 'Whoever dumped him there didn't do more than scrape a bit of a hole. I wonder if they were disturbed.'

Inspector Telford didn't think so. 'I know the spot we found him isn't all that far in distance from the road, but it's a road that doesn't go anywhere much. And it's hardly a scenic route, either, is it? My guess is that our joker had simply had enough. Look, he brings the body by car, right? Well, it's then got to be lugged over the fence, the barbed wire's got to be cut, and the body's got to be man-handled as far into the tip as possible. After that you've got to start digging a hole deep enough to bury it in – and with your bare hands. Look at those photographs. There's no sign that a spade was used. My bet is our laddie did the bare minimum and hoped for the best. And why not? It was pure chance that those workmen just happened to spot the body before somebody buried it for ever under a few tons of household rubbish.'

MacGregor reckoned that Inspector Telford had probably got it about right but he saw no point in telling him so. He changed the subject. 'You're assuming that the murder was committed elsewhere?'

Inspector Telford stared. 'Aren't you?'

'It's a possibility.'

'It's a dead cert, surely? You can't go killing somebody when you're both up to your knees in smelly tin cans and old potato peelings, even if your victim does happen to be starkers at the time. Besides, that's why the chief constable called you lot in. This job's not our pigeon. We just happen to be the dumping ground. The murder was definitely committed somewhere else, not in our bailiwick.'

MacGregor tapped his teeth with his pencil, a gesture designed to indicate deep thought. 'The choice of the rubbish tip indicates some local knowledge. You said yourself it was a bit off the beaten track. How would a stranger have known about it?'

'Oh, anybody could have known it was there,' insisted Inspector Telford, who had no intention of receiving this baby back again. 'It isn't a state secret and some days you can smell it for miles.'

MacGregor remained unconvinced but he knew better than to linger overlong on any one aspect, it being no distance at all to the end of Dover's tether. He contented himself with making an important looking note in his notebook and went on with his questions.

'Car tracks?' Inspector Telford shook his head. 'No, nothing like that. We had a good search round where the barbed wire fencing was cut, but we didn't find anything. No footprints or ire marks or bits of cloth that'd got snagged there. Mind you, we're only guessing anyhow that that's where the body was brought onto the dump.'

MacGregor permitted himself a little sigh. It was going to be one of *those* cases. Come to think of it, most of Chief Inspector Dover's were. 'Have we any idea yet how long the chap's been dead?'

'The doctor thought probably a long time. Weeks rather than days, he said. Months, maybe.'

'Years?'

'I don't think so.'

MacGregor closed his notebook. 'Well, I suppose we'll have a better idea after the P.M. There doesn't seem much we can do until then. You've been in touch with Missing Persons, have you? Just in case there's somebody who fits.'

'Yes, we've got all the routine checks in hand.' Inspector Telford leaned back in his chair and stretched himself. 'Mind you, I don't think they'll lead to much. If we're going to be able to identify the body as easily as that, why go to the trouble of disfiguring him?'

'The damage to the head and face could have been accidental.'

'And pigs might fly!'

'It could have been revenge.'

'Look, sergeant, the body was stripped of all its clothing. Even the teeth were removed. That chap had a complete set of dentures, top and bottom. Now, why take them out unless you want to stop us tracing him?'

'Fingerprints!'

There was a moment's panic and confusion before Inspector Telford realised that this was Dover now joining in the discussion. He'd been sitting there so long – slumped, silent and stuffed to the gills with cake – that everybody had forgotten about him.

'Er – fingerprints, sir? Er – fingerprints on what, exactly?'

'On the bloody corpse!' snarled Dover, who didn't suffer fools gladly.

Inspector Telford felt himself going red. 'Round the neck.

12

you mean, sir? Well, I don't think there's much chance of us getting . . .'

'Not round the neck, you loony!' rumbled Dover with mounting irritation. 'On his hands!'

'On his hands, sir?'

'You are checking 'em, aren't you?' demanded Dover.

'The corpse's fingerprints? Oh, yes, of course, sir.'

'Thank God for small mercies!' observed Dover with that charm of manner which made so many people long to take a blunt instrument to him. He picked up his bowler hat from a nearby chair and screwed it back lovingly on his head. 'I'll want to see the report the minute it comes in but don't disturb me. I've got a bit of quiet thinking to do. About the case!' he added savagely as he fancied he caught a look flickering across his sergeant's face. 'Now, what's this hotel you're supposed to have booked us into?'

'The Muncaster Arms, sir,' said Inspector Telford, trying to put an unworthy suspicion out of his mind. 'Er – there is just one small thing before you go, sir.'

'What?'

'We understand there's a go-slow on in the Fingerprint Bureau, sir. Something about the over-time rates. It's causing long delays. It may be weeks before we get a report on the dead man's fingerprints.'

''Strewth!' exploded Dover who always got very angry when he heard about other people downing tools and getting away with it. 'Some people want a bloody bomb putting under 'em!' He pulled himself to his feet and the caravan lurched unhappily as seventeen and a quarter stone of badly packaged fat slopped around in its interior. 'Oh, well, let me know when something breaks.' Dover was not unaware that some clouds have silver linings and he was more than willing to stay sitting on his backside and twiddling his thumbs for just as long as it took. And longer.

The manager of the Muncaster Arms, an unpretentious hostelry, had been well briefed by the local police. The pressures of a full-scale murder investigation being what they are, it was extremely unlikely that the two high-powered detectives from London would do more than use their rooms for a quick shave and a change of shirt. The manager was quite looking forward to all the excitement and it came as something of a disappointment to be confronted by a fat, bad-tempered slob in a filthy overcoat and a disgusting bowler hat demanding a DO NOT DISTURB notice for his door.

The manger of the Muncaster Arms never felt quite the same about policemen after that.

Dover remained in his bedroom for the rest of the day, emerging only every hour to belabour the sanitary arrangements and for one trip downstairs to the dining room where he partook of a hearty dinner. The following morning, however, revealed a much more animated scene. The chief inspector, refreshed (if not thoroughly bored) by some fifteen hours sleep, was almost up and raring to go.

'Does no harm to show your face once in a while,' he informed his long-suffering sergeant who was privileged to be in attendance at the levée. 'Keeps the idle beggars on their toes!'

'The local chaps seem very conscientious, sir,' said MacGregor, intent upon not looking at Dover standing there clad in nothing but a yellowing vest, one of the casualties of the War on Want. 'Actually, I've been rather impressed by the way they've handled things.'

'Fancy!' grunted Dover, dragging on a pair of voluminous matching underpants. 'Only trouble is, laddie, your opinions aren't worth the bloody paper they're written on.' He dragged his paunch in and managed to get the safety-pin fastened.

MacGregor turned the other cheek. 'Do you think we're up against one of those gangland killings, sir?'

'Don't talk so bloody wet!' Dover had never in his life failed to wallop the other cheek as well. 'You've been reading too many of those stupid thrillers.'

'It's got all the hallmarks of a professional job, though, don't you think, sir?' MacGregor was actually more concerned with clarifying his own ideas than soliciting Dover's. 'Cutting that barbed-wire fence so neatly, stripping the body and removing the teeth, burying it in a rubbish dump ... As Inspector Telford pointed out, with a modicum of luck we'd have never found out about the murder at all. Even now the odds are well against us being able to identify the victim. The whole business has a certan smoothness and coolness about it that's just not typical of your ordinary, run-of-the-mill murder.'

If there was one thing Dover didn't waste time on, it was arguments that he looked like losing. Skilfully he directed the discussion into less contentious channels. He held up the tumbler from his bedside table in a meaty, accusing paw. 'Have you nicked my teeth?' he demanded hotly.

It was at moments like this that Sergeant MacGregor was grateful that his dear mother couldn't see him. It would have broken her heart. 'I think you've already got them in, sir,' he said quietly, stifling a well-nigh overpowering impulse to ram the aforementioned dentures right down the abominable old fool's abominable throat.

Dover acknowledged the solution to his problem with an exploratory munch and an ill-natured grunt. 'A professional killer,' he pointed out, 'would have made one-hundred-percent bloody certain that we never found the body. He'd have used more men on the job, for a start.'

'But we don't know how many men, sir, were ...'

'Course we do! One! That's why the body wasn't taken a damned sight further into the rubbish tip and that's why it wasn't buried at least five or six feet down in a proper grave. The sloppy way it was done is proof positive it was a one-man job. He was too scared or too hurried or too bloody exhausted to make absolutely sure.'

Naturally MacGregor would rather have died than admit it, but it did strike him that there might be a tiny, mustard-seed size of sense in what Dover was saying. Not that he was prepared to abandon his own theory entirely. He still thought that there were definite indications that the dead body of the unknown man had been disposed of by somebody who was far from being either an amateur or a mug. Still, it was far too early to start theorising. What they needed at this stage was plenty of good, hard facts.

15

The telephone by Dover's bed rang and MacGregor hurried across to answer it while Dover put the finishing touches to his toilet.

'We'll be with you in five minutes!' MacGregor promised, the excitement of the news he'd just heard making him reckless. He put the phone down and turned to Dover who was moodily scraping at what looked like a lump of antique scrambled egg on his waistcoat. 'That was Inspector Telford, sir! There's been a new development! He's waiting for us at the Operations Room.'

Two

It was always a mistake to try and rush Dover, a fact
MacGregor remembered a little too late. Dover had two speeds
– dead slow and reverse – and so, instead of five, it was thirty-
five minutes before they made it to the Operations Room.

Dr Hone-Hitchcock, the eminent pathologist who had
performed the post mortem, was not best pleased. Assuming
that the detective in charge of the investigation would be
anxious to have the results without delay, Dr Hone-Hitchcock
had come round to deliver the gist of his report in person, confident that he would find Scotland Yard's Finest already hard
at work by half past eight in the morning.

'God damn it!' he exploded to Inspector Telford, holding his
watch up to his ear to make sure it was still going. 'I can't hang
around here all day! Where the hell is he?'

Inspector Telford had been wondering about that, too. 'They've
probably got held up in the traffic, sir,' he said soothingly.

'What traffic?' demanded Dr Hone-Hitchcock who had a
very fiery temperament for a pathologist. 'Muncaster's rush-
hour consists of six bicycles and a pram – and it was over three
hours ago.'

'Perhaps Mr Dover is pursuing some line of his own, sir, and
it's taking him a bit longer than they anticipated.'

'Balls!' retorted Dr Hone-Hitchcock with lamentable crudeness. 'He was still in bed when you rang through, wasn't he?'

'Well, maybe he's . . .'

Mercifully Inspector Telford's inventive powers were saved from further strain by the arrival of a car which drew up beside the caravan. It was the Great Man himself and Inspector Telford went out to welcome him and assist·in hoisting him up the caravan steps which were, as Inspector Telford freely admitted, a touch on the precipitous side for a man of Dover's build.

Dr Hone-Hitchcock had prepared quite a scholarly dissertation on his autoptical findings, but one look at Dover and he jettisoned it. 'I thought you'd like to have the P.M. results without delay,' he began when the introductions had been made and they'd got Dover settled in his chair.

Dover responded with his usual charm. 'No skin off my nose either way,' he grunted. 'Just don't go making a meal of it. The bare bones'll do me.' He sniggered delightedly at his own wit.

'The deceased,' said Dr Hone-Hitchcock shortly, 'was a middle-aged man. Flabby, over-weight and generally out of condition, thought there were no signs of any specific disease and no operation scars. I put his age about forty-five. At some time in his youth he broke his left arm, though I doubt if that's going to be of much help to you. Now, the cause of death. He was strangled from behind with a thin rope which was held tightly round his neck until life was extinct. Just held, not knotted. Time of death? Well, anything from four to eight weeks I'd guess, and he was placed in that hole on the rubbish dump within twenty-four hours of his death. Sorry I can't be more precise, but you know what it's like. By the way, there's no dental evidence. He hadn't got a tooth in his head. Complete clearance, top and bottom. He wore dentures, of course, but those are missing.'

Dover stirred restlessly. 'Strewth, some people didn't half like the sound of their own lah-di-dah voices! 'I thought you were supposed to have found something new?'

18

'I'd like first of all,' said Dr Hone-Hitchcock icily, 'to clear up the matter of the burns round the head and face.'

'Oh, big bloody deal!' muttered Dover, not quite as sotto voce as common politeness would have required.

Dr Hone-Hitchcock's nostrils flared. He was already promising himself he'd put a formal complaint in about this ill-mannered lout. Dr Hone-Hitchcock was a man of some eminence and his channels of communication went right up to the top. He'd cook this boor's goose for him, by God he would! 'The burns were caused by petrol. Lighter fuel, probably. A bottleful was poured over the head after death and then set alight. The burns were superficial but they did singe and blacken the skin, and most of the hair on the head and face was burnt off.'

There was a pause.

'Is that it?' asked Dover with a disparaging sniff.

Dr Hone-Hitchcock clenched his jaw. 'I did find this,' he said. 'In the stomach.'

With a flourish which, even in these unpropitious circumstances, couldn't help being a trifle theatrical, Dr Hone-Hitchcock placed a little blue object, the size of a smallish lump of sugar, on the table in front of Dover.

Dover poked at it despondently. 'What the hell is it?'

'I don't know.'

McGregor got down on his hands and knees to retrieve the little blue cube from the floor of the caravan. At least Dover's clumsiness ensured that the brains of the partnership managed to get a good look at the clue.

'I don't think it's a bead,' said MacGregor, pretending not to see that Dover wanted it back again. 'There's no hole for a string to go through.'

Dr Hone-Hitchcock turned gratefully to what appeared to be, if only in comparision with some, a veritable paragon of a policeman. 'There is that small protuberance on the one side,' he pointed out, 'and the small socket on the other. It looks to me as though, if we had two of them, we could sort of clip one into the other.'

It was Inspector Telford's turn to muscle in on the act. 'Poppets!' he announced triumphantly, taking the little blue artefact out of MacGregor's hand. 'Do you remember them?' They used to be all the rage. They were necklaces of beads that weren't strung together on a string but were slipped into each other. Woolworth's used to sell them. I remember my daughter had one. The thing was, you see, that you could fasten and unfasten them anywhere so you could make them into bracelets or have them any length you wanted.'

MacGregor took the bead back again. Trust the uniformed branch to start trying to play the detective!

'Mind you,' said Inspector Telford lamely, 'the things I'm thinking of didn't really look much like this. They were more sort of pearly and not as big.'

MacGregor took the bead over to the window. 'There are some letters stamped on it,' he said. 'Has anybody got a magnifying glass?'

It was several minutes before one of the policewomen found the Murder Bag which MacGregor had brought down from the Yard. It did contain a magnifying glass which was rather surprising as Dover had tipped most of the equipment out years ago to make room for his pyjamas and a spare pair of socks.

MacGregor squinted importantly through the lens. 'Yes,' he announced, 'three capital letters – R, H, and R – and the numbers two and five. Twenty-five, perhaps.' He looked round at his audience. 'What do you make of that?'

The policewoman who'd brought the Murder Bag provided the answer. 'It's Funny Money,' she said nonchalantly.

'What?'

'Funny Money?'

'What are you talking about, girl?'

'Who the hell asked her to go sticking her bloody nose in?'

In due course things calmed down sufficiently for the policewoman to explain, though she couldn't for the life of her see why it was necessary. Hadn't any of these clever dicks ever been to a holiday camp?

'A holiday camp?' repeated MacGregor incredulously. 'What

20

in heaven's name has this thing got to do with a holiday camp?'

Inspector Telford had no desire to go through all that screaming scene again. 'I'm sure WPC Kubersky will be only too willing to tell us, sergeant,' he said snubbingly, 'given half a chance.'

WPC Kubersky was. 'It's just that, when you go to one of these holiday camps, you know, they make you use these beads things instead of money. Like when you want to buy things or pay for extras. Or have a drink.'

MacGregor's scowl wouldn't have looked out of place on Dover's mug. 'But, why?'

WPC Kubersky's opinion of Scotland Yard was taking a dive. 'When they say "all-in",' she pointed out patiently, 'they don't mean "all-in", do they? You can't pay for everything in advance.'

'No,' agreed MacGregor, 'but . . .'

'There are bound to be extras, you know. Well, it stands to reason, doesn't it? Like incidentals.'

MacGregor reminded himself that the dratted girl was probably doing her best. He held up an authoritative hand so that he could get a word in. 'But why not use real money?'

Such naivety had WPC Kubersky reeling. Holy-Mary-Mother-of-God, they'd be asking her how many beans made five next! 'There must be dozens of reasons. It stops the staff getting their hands on hard cash you know, and then you can, like, disguise the real price of things. Like saying a bag of crisps costs five beads instead of forty-seven pence or whatever. And, if you want to put all your prices up, you don't have to, you know, go round changing all the tickets. Like you simply have to alter the rate of exchange. And then,' – WPC Kubersky might have had her shortcomings but she was wonderfully shrewd when it came to money – 'like abroad, in places like Italy, they never have any small change, do they? I reckon using these bead things is one way of getting round that problem.'

'Ah, Italy!' Inspector Telford clutched hopefully at one straw before it floated past him on the stream of WPC Kubersky's eloquence. 'These beads are used in Italian holiday camps, are they?'

'And Spanish ones,' said WPC Kubersky who was a much travelled girl. 'French, too, I shouldn't wonder. Lots of places.'

'But, abroad?'

'Oh, no' – WPC Kubersky got hold of the blue bead and examined it without the aid of the magnifying glass – 'in England, too. Like I bet this is English Funny Money. RHR – that could stand for Rankin's Holiday Ranches, couldn't it?'

'And what about the numbers?' asked Inspector Telford, anxious that this hitherto unsuspected luminary in their midst should be given every chance to shine.

'That'll be the value, sir. This blue bead is worth twenty-five of whatever.'

'Pence?' prompted Inspector Telford hopefully.

WPC Kubersky shook her head. These senior officers – they just hadn't got it, had they? 'More like other beads, sir,' she said. 'Green like, or red, or yellow. Are you ready for your coffee now, sir?'

The question had been addressed to Inspector Telford, but it was Dover who answered. 'Yes,' he said without a moment's hesitation. 'And see if you can rustle up a bite to eat, there's a good girl.'

Luckily MacGregor was capable of keeping his mind on higher things. 'Rankin's Holiday Ranches?' he mused. 'Well, it's a start. But what was the bead doing in the dead man's stomach? It's too big to have been swallowed accidentally, isn't it?' He turned to Dr Hone-Hitchcock. 'I suppose you didn't find any other foreign bodies inside him?'

'No, just this blue bead thing. It was all mixed up with the remains of the last meal he'd eaten. Venison, chips, baked beans and sprouts, followed by rice pudding and all washed down with about half a pint of beer. He'd consumed that lot about six or seven hours before he was killed. Maybe longer.'

'Venison?' said MacGregor. 'That's a bit unusual, isn't it? Could this bead thing have been connected with the venison?'

'How do you mean?'

MacGregor was really scraping the barrel. 'Well, suppose the young lady's wrong and it isn't this Funny Money stuff. It could be part of a cartridge, perhaps, or some sort of plastic tag on a carcase or a joint of meat.'

Dr Hone-Hitchcock looked at his watch and saw that he should have been somewhere else twenty minutes ago. Oh, well, he might as well be hung for a sheep and stay on for a cup of coffee. However, the spectacle of Dover perking up quite disgustingly as the coffee tray approached gave him pause. And when, in response to the stimulus of a plate of sticky cream cakes, Dover's animation became positively nauseating, Dr Hone-Hitchcock decided to cut his losses. He had been a Home Office pathologist for nigh on thirty years but there were some things even he couldn't stomach. He looked round for his hat.

Before he left, though, Dr Hone-Hitchcock did spare a moment to put young MacGregor on the right lines. 'That, sergeant,' he said, jabbing the blue bead with a magisterial finger, 'is a clue. In my considered opinion it could not have been swallowed accidentally nor was it consumed for nutritional purposes or because the deceased liked the taste. Ergo — it was ingested for some other reason, and that other reason was to provide a clue. The sort of thing I have in mind is a kidnapping, say. The victim knows he's going to be killed and he takes the only means available to him to provide some kind of a pointer to his murderer. It is the only explanation for the presence of that bead in the dead man's stomach.'

'You may be right, sir.'

Dr Hone-Hitchcock drew himself up. 'I am, sergeant,' he said confidently and took his leave.

Space in the caravan was at a premium and, as soon as the pathologist had gone, another of Inspector Telford's minions came bustling forward to take his place.

The minion handed MacGregor a sheet of paper. 'Here's the address of the Head Office of Rankin's Holiday Ranches, sarge,' he announced, modestly confident that this example of local initiative and efficiency would not pass unnoticed. 'We've already given 'em a buzz and warned 'em you're on your way.

Seems,' he added with the easy camaraderie of one professional to another, 'as though this blue-bead business might be going to open up a whole new ball game.'

Three

Sir Egbert Rankin was one of those people who preach delegation but who know that, if you want something done properly, you have to do it yourself.

When Dover and MacGregor came knocking at his door, figuratively speaking, he insisted upon seeing them himself, though a greatly daring confidential aide had been so bold as to suggest that it wasn't really necessary for the chairman and managing director of a multi-million corporation to ... Sir Egbert, however, was adamant. He hadn't built up Rankin's Holiday Ranches by the sweat of his brow and the spectacular proceeds of five years as a war time army quartermaster-sergeant to see it all fall apart now.

'Won't you at least have one of the company lawyers on hand, sir?'

Sir Egbert shot the cuffs of his silk shirt so that the diamond cuff links came into sight, and speared the button on his intercom.

His secretary flinched in panic at the other end.

'Them flat-feet still there?'

'Er – yes, sir.'

'Then what the 'ell are you waiting for? Wheel 'em in!'

Dover, at least, entered Sir Egbert's palatial office with the highest hopes. After the insalubrious environment of the Muncaster municipal rubbish dump almost anything would, of course, be an improvement, but it wasn't every day that rock-bottom brass like Dover was permitted to penetrate into the luxurious heartland of Big Business. The chief inspector had timed his arrival at the Park Lane offices with exquisite care: a trifle too late for morning coffee, of course, but exactly right for pre-lunch drinks.

It was therefore extremely gratifying for Dover to see that Sir Egbert was already priming the old digestive processes with a large scotch. Such, indeed, was Dover's elation that he covered the fifty yards or so of ankle-clinging carpet which led to the tycoon's desk without more than a faint whisper of protest.

MacGregor, on the other hand, was taking an intelligent interest in his surroundings. Although too young to remember the real thing, he had seen 'The Great Dictator' a couple of times on telly and fancied he knew what he was up against. Sir Egbert looked slightly more like Benito Mussolini than Charlie Chaplin, but he was clearly one of those financial giants, whose inferiority complexes even come king-sized.

Having reached the end of the long march, Dover and MacGregor lowered themselves into a couple of leather arm-chairs, the subservient height of which had been meticulously calculated by a whole clutch of psychologists.

'Drink?'

Dover accepted with alacrity, both ignorant of and indifferent to the fact that this was merely a ploy designed by experts to put him under an inhibiting sense of obligation to his host. MacGregor primly refused to be bought so cheaply.

Sir Egbert opened his case by denying, quite categorically, that there was any connection whatsoever between Rankin's Holiday Ranches and the little blue bead which had been removed from the dead man's stomach.

MacGregor pointed out that certain basic facts would be easy enough to verify.

'H'all right, h'all right!' said Sir Egbert, abandoning his

determination to fight this thing every inch of the way. 'So it looks like one of h'ours. That don't prove a blind thing.'

MacGregor, who'd never experienced any difficulty with his aspirates, became a touch patronising. Good heavens, Sir Egbert was nothing but a Philistine. What had he got apart from money? 'Oh, come along now, sir,' he twitted him gently. 'If it looks like one of your Holiday Ranch tokens, it must be one, mustn't it? Nobody's likely to be going around imitating them, are they?'

'That shows you know bugger-all about it!' retorted Sir Egbert. He knew – none better – all about sergeants and where they came in the pecking order. It was a pity that this snooty little bastard didn't. 'H'imitate 'em is just what folks do. All the bleeding time. Forgers?' He picked the blue bead up off his desk – ormolu and the size of a tennis court. 'If we didn't 'ave this Funny Money stuff manufactured to the 'ighest possible standards *and* run security checks like the Bank of England, we'd 'ave the world and his wife and 'is kids skinning the life out of us.'

'But these tokens can only be used in your holiday camps.'

''Oliday Ranches!' corrected Sir Egbert irritably. 'So what makes you think our clientele are different? They'd all take me to the cleaners if I didn't spend a fortune making it too difficult for 'em. We change the design and the colour and the size every year. And we give each 'Oliday Ranch its own individual set. The expense! We issue a complete new range of Funny Money every Easter, and by September there's 'alf-a-dozen crooked bastards flooding the market with their 'ome-made stuff. Anybody who can get his hands on a bit of plastic the right colour'll have a go. H'it makes you wonder if there's anybody honest left in the world.'

MacGregor singled out the one bit of this rigmarole which was of interest to him. 'Do you mean,' he said, narrowing his eyes in a way that would have had Dover rolling in the aisles if he'd noticed, 'that you can pin point when and where this blue bead was in use as Funny Money?'

'Ah!' said Sir Egbert, relaxing now that they'd reached the wheeler-dealer stage. 'It'll cost you.'

'Cost us?'

'You play ball with me and I'll play ball with you,' said Sir Egbert, not realising that he was nodding at a blind horse that wouldn't drink.

'I'm afraid I don't understand what you mean, sir.'

Sir Egbert's smile wavered as he was forced to spell things out. 'No publicity,' he explained. 'Stomachs, corpses, pile of rubbish – that's not the image we want our 'Oliday Ranches to project. You know what stupid bastards people are. Give 'em a story like that and they'll think we choked the poor sod to death. And then they'll decide to give Rankin's 'Oliday Ranches a miss this year. Believe me, I've seen it all before. If we don't make like Caesar's wife, it starts showing up in the books.'

MacGregor, being paid by the long-suffering tax payer, took a somewhat Olympian view of the trials and tribulations of the market place. 'I'm afraid we have no control over the news media, sir,' he said. 'Besides, I thought any publicity was good publicity.'

'If it was,' Sir Egbert observed sourly, 'we'd be marketing a rat poison called Rankin, wouldn't we?'

Dover belched loudly in his chair. His glass was empty and his eyes were glazed. Both MacGregor and Sir Egbert stared a little anxiously at him. Dover pulled himself together. 'Well, lesh get on with it!' he exhorted them crossly.

Sir Egbert decided not to hang about. The whisky he kept specially for his guests was cheap and nasty, but extremely potent. Some people had even experienced temporary blindness after imbibing a mere soupçon over the recommended dose. Sir Egbert got up from his desk and went across to open the huge wall safe he kept concealed behind a rather second rate Giotto.

The various models of Funny Money were preserved in sealed trays of transparent plastic, labelled carefully and meticulously in Sir Egbert's own fair hand. After all, these coloured beads did represent real money and Sir Egbert liked to think he'd made it from demob suit to Savile Row in two years flat simply by taking good care of the pennies.

The blue bead was soon identified. It was that season's model.

'And to which Holiday Ranch, sir?'

Sir Egbert consulted a chart. 'Bowerville-by-the-sea.'

'Bowerville-by-the-sea?' repeated MacGregor as he wrote the name down in his notebook. 'Where's that, sir?'

'Northumberland,' said Sir Egbert with every confidence. 'Or Yorkshire. Somewhere up there.'

MacGregor frowned. 'In either case it's a long way from Muncaster where the body was found.'

'Motorways,' opined Sir Egbert. In his line of business communications were important. 'From anywhere to anywhere in a matter of minutes.'

'I suppose the best thing,' said MacGregor, more or less thinking aloud, 'would be for us to have a word with the manager. And, indeed, anybody else who was up there at the relevant time.' He turned to Sir Egbert. 'I suppose somebody will be able to let us have the names and addresses of all the staff and the holiday-makers, sir? We may need to interview the lot before we're through.'

Dover, who could still taste that whisky, hadn't been feeling too bright even before this appalling prospect opened up before him. ''Strewth!' he ejaculated weakly. It was, as things turned out, his most valuable contribution to the discussion.

'H'easy,' said Sir Egbert. 'Course, if you go up to Bowerville-by-the-sea, you'll find the manager and some of the staff still there. Not the part-timers, of course. They're only employed for the summer months.'

'Is the Holiday Ranch still open, sir?' MacGregor was surprised. 'At this time of year?'

'We can't afford to 'ave a capital asset standing idle for four months out of twelve,' explained Sir Egbert with slightly more difficulty than usual. The thought of fluctuating profits did tend to make him over-emotional. 'Not these days. Then there's our workers. They want regular employment.'

'But do you get holiday-makers in November or February?'

'There's old-age pensioners,' said Sir Egbert. 'We offer very competitive terms and most of 'em don't suit central 'eating anyhow. Then there's people taking a winter break, and conferences. That's where the big money is. A couple of really big conferences that take over an entire Ranch and we're laughing. We turn the ballrooms into conference 'alls and the gymnasiums into h'exhibition centres and we can provide dozens of smaller, committee-type rooms as well. Nothing's too much trouble. They're big spenders, you see. Drink the bar dry every night, if you're lucky.'

'Really?' said MacGregor who was always willing to have his horizons widened.

'Of course,' Sir Egbert went on, 'mostly we deal with smaller groups. You can 'ave as much or as little accommodation as you want, you know. We get 'undreds of 'em. Trade unions and toy soldier collectors and women's lib and folk dancing and regimental reunions – you name 'em, we've 'ad 'em.' Sir Egbert looked up. He was not the man to miss a golden opportunity. 'I'll give you a few of our brochures,' he said. 'Maybe some of your police organisations . . . Special terms, naturally.'

'Thank you, sir,' said MacGregor, absent-mindedly but still polite. 'Actually, I was wondering if I'd got the picture absolutely straight. This piece of Funny Money which was found in the stomach of the dead man came – and could only have come – from your Holiday Ranch at Bowerville-by-the-sea.'

'He could have picked it up in the street,' said Sir Egbert, still anxious not to have his organisaton too closely involved. 'Or somebody could 'ave give it to him. There's no proof he was ever anywhere near Bowerville.'

'Oh, there are numerous possibilities, I agree, sir, but for the moment I think we've got to proceed on the theory that the unknown dead man has some connection with your Holiday Ranch at Bowerville-by-the-sea. He must have been trying to tell us something when he swallowed that blue bead.'

'You think he was a holiday-maker there?'

'That seems the likeliest explanation.'

Sir Egbert sank back in his chair with a faint whistle. 'It'll run into thousands,' he prophesied. 'Thousands and thousands. Most of 'em only stay one week, and Bowerville-by-the-sea can take three 'undred. You'll be at it till Doomsday.'

Dover twitched unhappily but MacGregor, the bloom of youthful enthusiasm still upon his cheek, refused to be daunted. 'Oh, it won't be as bad as all that, sir. We can eliminate all the women for a start, and there'll be all the men who are obviously in the wrong age group. That should cut the numbers down quite considerably. We're used to jobs of this type, sir. I think we have quite a reasonable chance of identifying our dead man, and then we can start going after his murderer.' MacGregor stood up. 'Thank you for sparing us so much of your time, sir.'

'My pleasure,' said Sir Egbert, watching with interest as MacGregor began to assist Dover out of his armchair. Sir Egbert hadn't been able to make Dover out at all. Could such a dopey-looking lump really be a high-powered detective? God knows, Sir Egbert wasn't fussy about the quality of the hired help – he'd learned not to be over the years – but even he'd think twice about giving this one a job sorting out the pig swill.

MacGregor had got Dover almost to the door before Sir Egbert mentioned that there was a favour he wanted to ask. He'd been having second thoughts about this business of the publicity. 'The blue bead is still my property, I believe, sergeant.'

'That's a debatable point, sir. If somebody bought it off you . . .'

'I think you'll find that, technically, we lease the things rather than sell 'em.'

'In any case, we shall have to hang on to it for the time being,' said MacGregor, contriving to prop Dover up against the wall while he got the door open. 'It's vital evidence.'

'You'll let me 'ave it back in the end, though?'

MacGregor thought that this could probably be arranged.

When the door had finally closed behind his visitors, Sir Egbert let his face relax into a hopeful grin. A glass case? A velvet cushion, perhaps? Uniformed guards and a fifty-pence entrance fee? Yes, properly handled, that little blue bead could put Bowerville-by-the-sea and its Holiday Ranch right on the map! But why stop at Bowerville? It could boost the takings of every single Rankin's Holiday Ranch in the country. Which of his rivals could boast such a treasure? Rankin's would be the only blooming chain in the business that'd got a piece of its Funny Money found inside the stomach of a murdered man!

Sir Egbert turned his eyes piously in the general direction of that Great Travel Agent in the sky. Dear God, make it one of those really nasty, sordid, sexy murders . . . *please*!

Meanwhile there were still things needing to be done down here in this vale of tears. Sir Egbert, diamond cuff links flashing, dived for his intercom button again.

Four

Thus alerted by his head office, the manager and herd boss of Rankin's Bowerville-by-the-sea Holiday Ranch had ample time to take the usual precautions. A few account books were hidden, a few faces warned to stay out of sight, a few skeletons popped back into their cupboards. It was the routine stuff. After all, if it wasn't Customs and Excise poking around, it was somebody from Health and Social Security or a factory inspector or a busybody about the VAT. Establishment snoopers never sleep and this new lot were exceptional only in that they were travelling by train and not in their own chauffeur-driven limousine.

When Dover and MacGregor finally emerged from the gritty embrace of British Rail they found a mini-bus from the Ranch waiting for them. MacGregor, blessed with ideas above his station, would have preferred transport which was not plastered with vulgar and garish advertisements, but naturally Dover didn't give a damn. His feet were killing him and, as long as he didn't have to walk, he was easy.

'I don't know,' he confided to MacGregor as they bowled along by the side of a sullen, steel-gray sea, 'how much longer I'm going to be able to carry on.'

MacGregor had heard all this a thousand times before. 'Really, sir?'

'I'm not at all well, you know,' said Dover, aiming for a pathetic note. 'It's my stomach. It's playing me up something cruel. Well, you saw that for yourself. In and out of that toilet like a bloody jack-in-the-box.'

MacGregor had not forgotten. Nor, he suspected, had the other passengers in their compartment who had been privileged to share in Dover's running commentary on his troubles. 'Perhaps it was all those railway pies you had, sir. Or the sausage rolls. They did look rather greasy.'

'I reckon I've caught a chill,' said Dover miserably.

'Pastry can be rather indigestible at times, sir.'

'Indigestible?' snarled Dover. 'I'm not talking about a bit of belly-ache or a touch of the wind, laddie!' He flinched slightly as a sudden flurry of sleet rattled the windows of the minibus. 'It's the bloody trots I've got, and don't you forget it.'

'No, sir.'

'I'll tell you something else too,' said Dover on the principle that a trouble shared is a trouble halved. 'If we don't get to wherever it is we're going pretty damn quick, we'll be in trouble. Get it?'

MacGregor got it all right. He stared out at the bleak, mist-enshrouded sea-scape and tried to think of something to distract Dover's mind. 'It's decent of the Holiday Ranch to offer us accommodation for the night, isn't it, sir? I hadn't appreciated how far away from everywhere it is. Quite isolated, really.'

'Bloody concentration camp!' muttered Dover morosely. 'Waste of time, too. That blue bead thing isn't going to lead us anywhere. Stands to reason.'

'It's the only clue we have, sir.'

A fat lot Dover cared. 'Somebody'll turn up sooner or later and report him missing,' he said. 'Until then,' – he brightened up at the prospect – 'there's nothing we can do except sit back and bloody wait.'

'There we are, gents!' The driver of the minibus gesticulated ahead into the gloom and the spray. 'There's Rankin's!'

MacGregor, who had exceptionally keen eyesight, could just make out a miserable collection of huts huddled together on the very edge of the beach. Once they must have been brightly painted but now their colours had faded to a dispirited pastel. Here and there the smooth surface of a concrete roadway gleamed through the driving rain.

It was another five minutes before Dover and MacGregor reached their destination and debussed in front of a larger than average hut. It's walls were covered in notices – clear, stark and aggressive. NO PARKING, they said, and PRIVATE. RANCH STAFF ONLY, they snarled. NO ADMITTANCE. STRICTLY OUT OF BOUNDS. ALL PASSES TO BE SHOWN. ADMINISTRATION BUILDING.

'Through there, gents!' The minibus driver helpfully indicated a door labelled KEEP OUT! THIS MEANS YOU!!

Dover and MacGregor, any reluctance to intrude where they might not be welcome being overcome by the way the wind was sand-blasting the skin off their faces, went inside. They found themselves in a small corridor along which, thanks to a cunning arrangement of steel filing cabinets, they were obliged to progress in single file. Captain Maguire had been manager for six years, and nobody lasts that long by taking chances. If he'd thought he could get away with it, he'd have installed man-traps, too, and hung buckets of boiling oil from the ceiling.

'Ha, ha!' Captain Maguire hailed them when they'd finally penetrated his defences. 'I've been expecting you!' He dropped his life-preserver back in the desk drawer. 'Take a pew! And *shut up*, Attila!' The snarling Doberman Pinscher eased back fractionally on the heavy chain which held him riveted to the wall. 'Now, then,' – Captain Maguire swung back to his visitors – 'how do you take it?'

'Er – take it, sir?' MacGregor was more concerned with getting Dover settled in a chair which looked as though it might stand his weight. 'Take what?'

'The usquebaugh, old son!' said Captain Maguire, vexed at having to explain the facts of life to a grown man. 'The poteen! The fire-water! The cup that inebriates!' He flourished a large bottle.

'Ah,' said MacGregor, catching on at last, 'you mean whisky, sir?'

It was three o'clock in the afternoon.

Captain Maguire's face darkened. 'You're not a teetotaller, are you?' he asked in tones so menacing that the Doberman bared his teeth again.

'I'm not!' said Dover, anxious that the interview shouldn't get off on the wrong foot. 'And I take it straight!'

'Good man!' Captain Maguire slopped a generous ration of the amber liquid into a half-pint tankard. 'You're a chappie after my own heart! But what about Little Lord Fauntleroy here? We can't leave him out in the cold. Would he prefer a drop of the old ruin?'

Dover was already expanding like a flower in the sheer warmth of Captain Maguire's welcome. At least this fellow kept a drop of decent booze. 'Oh, forget him!' he advised. 'He's still wet behind the ears.'

'He's got to learn to hold his liquor, my old darling,' said Captain Maguire, eyeing MacGregor dubiously. 'There's no room at the top these days for a laddie who can't keep a clear head when all about are losing theirs.'

Dover sank to hitherto unexplored depths of disloyalty. 'He'll go puking all over your office,' he warned, getting bored with the discussion. 'He doesn't drink anything stronger than tea. Besides,' – he passed his glass back over the desk for a refill – 'he's got to take notes.'

Captain Maguire filled up Dover's tankard and his own. 'Oh, one of your pen-pushing brigade, is he? Say no more! I know the breed. Well,' – he paused to dry off his moustache – 'let's get down to the nitty-gritty. Sir Bert gave me a tinkle but the poor old sod wasn't at his most coherent. Bends the old elbow a bit, you know. Still, none of us is perfect.'

Sycophantly Dover agreed and unbuttoned his overcoat. It was getting very hot in the office. 'They found this dead man, you see,' he explained. 'On that rubbish dump. Couple of days ago.'

'I read about it. What a way to pass through the pearly gates, eh?'

36

'When they slit him open, they found this blue bead thing inside.' Dover snapped his flabby fingers and MacGregor obediently produced what could, with a modicum of luck, be the chief exhibit in a murder trial and gave it to Captain Maguire.

'Yes, it's one of ours,' declared Captain Maguire when he'd managed to get both eyes focussed on the target at the same time. 'It's a Giggle.'

MacGregor, who was indeed taking notes, looked up. He was rather shocked at such levity. Captain Maguire was, after all, wearing a Brigade of Guards tie.

'And so worth twenty-five Titters,' Captan Maguire went on with a grin. 'Twenty-five Titters,' he chanted, 'equals one Giggle. Five Giggles equals one Snigger. Ten Sniggers equals one Guffaw.'

'I'm afraid I don't quite follow you, sir.'

'Actually, sonnie boy, that's the idea. For you not to understand it, I mean.' Captain Maguire got a small cigar box out of one of the desk drawers and tipped the contents out with a careless hand. Blue, yellow, green and red beads went skittering in all directions. 'The token things we use instead of the genuine spondulicks,' he explained. 'I thought Sir Bert was supposed to have briefed you up in the old Metropolis.'

'I hadn't appreciated it was quite so elaborate, sir.'

'Got to be, old son.' Captain Maguire made several genuine but unsuccessful efforts to pick the Funny Money up and put it back in the cigar box. 'Otherwise even the stupid buggers we get here would twig what was going on. As it is, most of 'em go their entire bleeding holiday without ever working it out that our ice creams cost two and a half times as much as they do outside. Still,' – he leaned back and groped around in a cupboard for a fresh bottle – 'it gives the poor sods something to think about, doesn't it? Takes their minds off the weather and the plumbing.'

'Don't the holiday-makers complain, sir?'

'Of course they complain, boyo! They complain endlessly. About everything.' Captain Maguire dropped the dead man in his waste-paper basket. 'Mind you, they enjoy it. Like traffic jams and strikes at Heathrow. It brings a touch of glamour into their grotty lives. Of course,' – he tossed the top off the new bottle in the general direction of his ashtray – 'occasionally one of the more persistent and bloody-minded bleeders goes too far and actually manages to penetrate right in here. Well, they get precious little change out of me! The last bolshie-type bastard who had the damned gall to raise his voice in my office got the toe of my boot up his backside before I set the dog on him.'

'Good heavens!' said MacGregor.

'Threatening to sue,' added Captain Maguire proudly. 'Nineteenth this year. All talk, though.'

Captain Maguire was so clearly a man after Dover's own heart that the chief inspector felt he wanted to do something to show his appreciation. He addressed MacGregor in an unaccustomed burst of generosity. 'Show him the picture!'

'Are you sure, sir?'

'Course I'm sure!' snapped Dover, irritated that his munificence should thus be questioned. 'You want the joker identified, don't you?'

MacGregor got the photograph which had been taken of the dead man out of his wallet and reluctantly passed it over.

'Christ Almighty!' exclaimed Captain Maguire blinking.

Dover leaned forward. 'Do you recognise him?'

'His own mother wouldn't! What the devil's happened to him?'

'He was burnt, sir, and of course his teeth have been removed.'

'Jesus!' Captain Maguire handed the photograph back and restored his shattered nerves in the only way he knew how. 'Not that it makes much odds,' he said as his second mouthful hit the spot. 'I never look at their faces. They're all just bundles of pound notes to me, and I've every intention of keeping it that way. God, you'd go round the bend if you started thinking of a smelly shower like that as human beings.'

Dover deposited his empty tankard with a thump on the desk. 'It doesn't have to be a holiday-maker,' he pointed out with unusual perspicacity. 'It could be somebody on the staff.'

'I'd still need a recognisable face, old son.'

'A middle-aged man, sir,' prompted MacGregor. 'False teeth. Darkish hair. About five foot eight. A bit overweight.'

Captain Maguire shook his head. 'It could be anybody.'

'Think!' urged Dover, almost as if he cared. 'Has anybody gone missing recently? Round about a couple of months or so ago? Cleared off without giving notice or saying anything?'

Captain Maguire shrugged his shoulders. 'They're always doing that,' he objected. 'Idle lot of buggers! Talk about here today and gone tomorrow. I can't think of anybody who'd fit the bill, word of honour. Actually, we don't employ all that many men, you know. The cleaners are all women, and most of the catering staff. Girls in the office, too.'

'All right, the holiday-makers, then! Anybody leaving in suspicious circumstances there? Like without paying their bloody bill?'

Captain Maguire looked at Dover as though unable to believe his ears. No wonder civilisation as we know it was crumbling if coppers were as dim as this! 'You must be joking, old man!' he said. 'Look, you don't think somebody who's as fly as old Sir Bert is going to let sodding little clerks and factory hands welsh on him, do you? For God's sake! They have to pay for everything in advance, my old china! Cash on the nail or ten working days if they offer one of their grotty little cheques. After that, who cares? The buggers are on their own. If they don't want to stick it out to the bitter end, that's their affair. All a premature departure means to Rankin's bleeding Holiday Ranches is a fraction more profit. Christ, one of the great unwashed goes missing and you reckon I call out the watch? No way, old son! The only time we take any action is if they depart with any of our furniture and fittings which, if you've seen the way our so-called bunk houses are equipped, is not a frequent occurrence.'

MacGregor was still reluctant to throw in the towel. 'Are you sure you can't help us, sir?'

'Frightfully sorry, old chap. But hasn't your stiff got any

family or chums? Why hasn't his wife reported him missing?'

'She probably croaked him,' said Dover who believed that murder and matrimony were just two sides of the same coin.

MacGregor sighed. 'Then we shall just have to mount a full-scale, nation-wide enquiry, I'm afraid. I shall want the names and addresses, sir, of all the people who've been here on holiday since Easter, and of all your employees for the same period.'

'Hell's steaming teeth!' exclaimed Captain Maguire. His secretary wasn't going to take kindly to this, paperwork not being her strong point nor, indeed, what she'd been hired for. 'It'll take years! Can't you narrow it down a bit?'

'I suppose we could ignore anybody who's only been here in the last month,' said MacGregor, not too enthusiastically. 'The chap's been dead at least that long.'

'But, if you've got the date of death, couldn't you manage with people who were here round about that time?'

Unfortunately MacGregor was one of those people who believe in doing a job well. It was a philosophy to which Dover also subscribed, with the proviso that it was somebody else who did the work.

'I'm afraid, sir,' said MacGregor, 'that would be making too big an assumption. The time the blue bead was acquired may have no connection at all with the time of death. However, we'll start with the people who were staying here round about that period. We may strike lucky and not have to bother with the rest.

Captan Maguire still wasn't very happy. Damn it all, it was only last week that Doris had been yowling on that she couldn't be at it twenty-four hours a day, seven days a week. 'It's going to put my staff to one hell of a lot of trouble, sergeant.'

MacGregor sighed. Captain Maguire seemed to be making a great deal of fuss about nothing but, since the police were always being urged to be nice to the general public ... He leafed back through the pages of his notebook. He couldn't agree to any skimping that would jeopardise the investigation but he'd got this idea at the back of his mind that there was something somewhere which might economise on the amount of time and ...

'Venison,' said Dover, his devotion to things comestible finally paying off.

MacGregor could have spat.

'Venison?' Captain Maguire's face brightened. 'Why the hell didn't you say that before?'

'I was just about to, sir,' said MacGregor, going pink with mortification. Well, it was true. Another second or so and he would have remembered all about the . . . Oh, it was sickening, it really was! If there was one thing worse than having Dover sitting around all day on his back-side doing damn-all, it was having the disgusting old fool opening his stupid trap and sticking his oar in. 'The post mortem revealed that the dead man had eaten some venison shortly before he was killed,' MacGregor went on hurriedly, trying to regain control of the interview. 'Does that help?'

'I'll say!' Captain Maguire plunged into action with typical military dash and vigour. 'Doris!' he bawled. 'Dig out that bill from Cooper's for that venison they flogged us, there's a good girl! Some time in October, I think. Bring it round when you've found it, eh? We'll be in the bar.' He snatched up the heavy riding crop without which he never ventured outside his office and looked across at Dover. 'Come on, old dear!' he urged hospitably. 'Show a leg there! We're wasting good drinking time.'

Five

Captain Maguire settled himself down at one end of the bar in the Keir Hardie Saloon as though he'd been drinking there for years, which he had. It was not at all clear why he had bothered to move out of his office. He can't have been compelled by financial considerations as he chalked up his alcoholic consumption to his employers wherever it took place. It can hardly have been the desire for convivial company either as the only other occupants of the saloon were a depressed-looking couple who'd arrived for a Weeke of Mediaevale Feastinge. No, the truth was that Captain Maguire was something of a law unto himself – and Dover for one wouldn't have had it any other way.

'Lucky you mentioned that venison, old chap,' Captain Maguire said as he watched Dover hoist seventeen and a quarter stone of over-indulgence onto a bar stool. 'It's going to save a hell of a lot of trouble. And I do mean *terrouble!*'

Dover's interest was temporarily occupied by watching the barman deposit, without a word being spoken by anybody, a row of doubles in front of his latest customers. 'Ah,' said Dover vaguely and then, although completely unpractised in the art, caught the barman's eye. 'Bring Sunny Jim, here, a tomato juice!' he ordered grandly, and helped himself quickly to his sergeant's whisky.

MacGregor cringed and prayed without success that the floor would open and swallow him.

Meanwhile Captain Maguire, having lubricated his own larynx with the vin du pays of Bonnie Scotland, was continuing with the conversation. 'If it had been sheep's brains,' he averred, his enunciation only slightly slurred, 'or tripe and onions, we'd have been right up the creek. We dish them out every other day, but – venison – that was a one-off job. Old Cooper offered me a few pounds at a very reasonable rate. Well, it was either that or have the stuff go rotten on him. We only just caught it in time. Next day even Attila turned his nose up at it.' A faint alarm bell came tinkling through the swirling mists of booze. 'I say,' he whispered hoarsely, 'this joker of yours – he didn't die of food poisoning, did he?'

Dover hastened to reassure his new-found friend. 'Shtrangled,' he said, getting his tongue round the word at the third time of asking.

'Good-oh!' Captain Maguire summoned up another round of the same in celebration. 'Well, like I said, we served this venison stuff one Saturday lunch. Pearls before swine, old man! You should have heard 'em. Still, they ate it in the end, it being that or nothing. I don't know what they were whining about. It looked palatable enough to me. Anyhow, I never repeated the experiment. I get enough aggro in this job without going round manufacturing it.'

Since Dover appeared unwilling to pursue the matter further, MacGregor fastidiously dabbed a trace of tomato juice off his upper lip and took up the questioning. 'So, what you're saying, sir, is that on one specific Saturday this season, you served venison. To your staff and the holiday-makers?'

Captain Maguire was much amused. 'Catch my staff eating that muck!'

'Then, whoever ate the venison would be a holiday-maker?'

'I should think so. I reckon we had that venison about a couple of months ago. Does that fit in with the time your chap cashed his chips? Still, as soon as Doris gets here with the files we'll be able to sort out all the details.'

44

MacGregor began to feel they were making progress at last. 'And you'll be able to let me have a list of the holiday-makers who were staying here at the time, sir?'

'Nothing simpler!' Captain Maguire raised an eyebrow and, twenty yards away, the barman reached for the whisky bottle. 'Actually, from what I remember, most of the paying customers were old-age pensioners that weekend. Special out-of-season rates.'

MacGregor shook his head. 'Our chap wasn't an old-age pensioner, sir. Far too young.'

'Oh, there'd be a few others here as well, I expect,' said Captain Maguire indifferently. He unscrewed the empty glass from Dover's hand and replaced it with a full one. 'Dirty weekenders, if nothing else.'

As has already been hinted, Doris as an employee was more accommodating than efficient, and by the time she finally arrived in the Keir Hardie Saloon with a sufficiency of books and documents, MacGregor was the only one capable of taking much interest. He ordered the girl a cherry brandy on the house and settled down to sort through the dog-eared pile she'd dumped disconsolately on the bar counter.

Captain Maguire, the back still ramrod though the eye was glassy, had been trying to induce a paralytic Dover to join him in some bawdy, tap-room ditty, the tempo of which he was thrashing out with his riding crop. When Doris appeared, however, he promptly let Dover sag back into his amorphism and gave all the attention of which he was capable to the girl.

The thing took some sorting out but, in the end, MacGregor flattered himself that he'd more or less got the picture. On the weekend that there'd been venison on the menu, the Bowerville-by-the-sea Holiday Ranch must have been nine-tenths empty. According to MacGregor's researches there were only two groups in residence and no individual holiday-makers at all.

Of the two group bookings, MacGregor felt that he could dispense with the Golden Lads and Lassies Sodality from Wootle. They were a party of senior citizens — thirty-seven ladies and three men — who had spent ten fun-filled days at Bowerville-by-the-sea. In addition to the pensioners themselves, there had been a couple of volunteer female handlers and the coach driver. The coach driver was a possibility as the dead man at Muncaster, but MacGregor didn't really fancy him. The Golden Lads and Lassies had presumably returned without difficulty to Wootle and MacGregor felt certain that even they would have noticed if their driver had gone missing.

The other lot looked more promising. This was an organisation called the Dockwra Society, with headed notepaper to prove it. Through their Honorary Secretary they had booked four adjacent chalets (or bunk-houses as they were known at Rankin's) which had provided them with accommodation for seven people in single rooms plus an extra room in which they could have their meetings.

MacGregor turned to Captain Maguire for enlightenment.

'Ah,' said Captain Maguire, removing only his eyes from the fair Doris. 'Four bunk-houses, eh?'

'You remember?'

'No.'

MacGregor, who had picked up more of Dover's methods of interrogation than he would have cared to admit, gave Captain Maguire quite a rough shake. 'It says in the file,' he insisted, 'that they were situated in Shinwell Square.'

'So?'

'Well, where's that?'

'Third on the right off Barbara Castle Prospect,' said Captain Maguire promptly and without rancour. He could have mentioned — but didn't — that these names harked back to the period when Sir Egbert was working for his K.

'I should like to see it.'

Captain Maguire waved a hospitable hand. 'Be my guest.'

MacGregor realised that, where Captain Maguire was concerned, he was already working on borrowed time. Quite apart from the personal magnetism of the nubile Doris, fresh rations of whisky were already wending their way down the bar and it wasn't to be expected that the Captain would devote much more of his time to investigating a murder. 'You only seem to have the name and address of the secretary of the Dockwra Society, sir. What about the other members? Haven't you got any information about them?'

'Always deal with the boss, old chap,' said Captain Maguire thickly. 'He's the one with the money.'

There is absolutely no doubt that MacGregor would have pursued the matter much further if Dover hadn't chosen this moment to topple off his stool. What with dragging Dover out of the bar, transporting him across to his bunk-house in a fortuitously handy wheelbarrow, putting him to bed and then returning to the Keir Hardie Saloon only to find that Captan Maguire and Doris had skipped it, even MacGregor eventually felt it was time to call it a day. Outside, as he already knew to his cost, it was pitch dark and raining cats and dogs. Even if he succeeded in locating Shinwell Square he wouldn't be able to see anything. He decided he might as well behave like everybody else and forget about the whole sorry business until the morning.

MacGregor treated himself to a dry sherry and then went to have his evening meal in a dining room as large, as uninviting and as chilly as an aircraft hanger. At the next table a dozen or so Mediaevale Feasters slumped miserably over their deep-freeze trout and chips while, away at the far end, a shop steward was trying to persuade the waitresses that their go-slow had gone unnoticed and that they all ought to come out on a proper strike.

The television in the Cow-poke's Parlour was out of order.

And it was still raining.

At eight o'clock MacGregor retired to bed in the bunk-house he was sharing with Dover. He gritted his teeth and settled down to twelve hours in a hard, damp bed and to a symphony of snores, grunts and snorts which came wafting from down the corridor. When William Schwenk Gilbert had talked about the policeman's lot, thought MacGregor bitterly at 2 a.m., he didn't know the bloody half of it.

Rankin's Holiday Ranches didn't run to serving breakfast in

bed but, luckily for Dover, detective sergeants from Scotland Yard did.

'I thought you'd bloody well emigrated!' shouted Dover from his bedroom as MacGregor staggered up the bunk-house steps with his tray. 'I suppose you've had your bloody breakfast,' he added as MacGregor entered his bedroom.

MacGregor, not trusting himself to speak, placed the tray on Dover's knees.

Dover was sitting up with his overcoat wrapped round his shoulders. "Strewth, what a dump!' he grumbled as he picked up a piece of bacon in his fingers. 'And people actually pay good money to stay here?'

MacGregor perched himself on the bedside chair and tried not to look. Dover – bloated, hung-over, white of face and red of eye – was not the sort of sight any fastidious person would choose to contemplate.

But our natural sympathy for MacGregor mustn't blind us to the fact that Dover, too, had his problems. Like what the hell happened last night. He'd got a dim feeling that somebody somewhere had made some progress and, since he was pretty sure it wasn't him, he wanted to slam the brakes on before things went too far. Better that the identity of the dead man on the rubbish tip should remain a mystery for ever than that this bloody little infant prodigy he'd been saddled with should come up with the answer. First, though, he had to find out how the land lay.

Dover soaked a piece of buttered toast in his tea. That was the trouble with your National Health teeth – they were worth bugger-all when it came to munching. 'I reckon,' said Dover in a spray of soggy crumbs, 'we'd better have a recap.'

It didn't fool MacGregor for a second, of course, but he pulled out his notebook. Actually, he'd be quite glad to run over things again, just to clarify his own thoughts. 'I think we're beginning to make some headway, sir.' He was slightly surprised to realise that this was true. Somehow one didn't associate making headway with cases in which Dover was involved. 'I think we can work on the assumption that our Mr

X was here at the Holiday Ranch, in some capacity or another, shortly before he was killed. The piece of Funny Money – that's the blue bead, you remember, sir – and the venison he'd consumed at his last meal virtually prove that. Indeed, sir, I think we may conclude that he deliberately swallowed the blue bead in order to lead us here.' MacGregor paused. 'Of course, that implies he knew he was going to be killed and that he had some time to think about leaving a clue.'

Dover spooned up a lump of marmalade from his top sheet. 'We still don't know who the blighter is,' he groused, as willing as ever to look on the dark side.

MacGregor agreed. 'But we are narrowing the field down, sir.' He consulted his notes. 'Venison was served here at midday on Saturday the fourteenth of October, which fits in well with what the post mortem came up with as the probable time of death. So we have our unidentified man eating his last meal here at the Holiday Ranch on that Saturday.' MacGregor stopped speaking to let all this sink in. It didn't do to overload Dover's brain with too many facts all at once.

After a few moment's delay, the oracle uttered. 'Humph,' said Dover.

'The next thing, sir, is that we have to ascertain who was here at the Holiday Ranch at that particular time. Of course we can discount anybody who's been seen alive and well since that time. They can hardly be our unknown dead man, can they?'

As jokes go, this one hit rock bottom like a lead pancake.

'Yack, yack, yack!' chanted Dover wearily.

'Captain Maguire and I have virtually eliminated all the staff who were around at the critical time, sir.'

Dover was scowling again.

MacGregor, a devout believer in the Scotland Yard myth that there were times when Dover couldn't even remember his own name, hastened to elucidate. 'Captain Maguire is the manager of this Holiday Ranch, sir.'

Dover was not inhibited by gratitude. 'Oh, *him*!' he commented viciously, fully aware to whom he was indebted for his present splitting head and queasy stomach.

'That just leaves us with the two groups who were staying here, sir. A party of senior citizens, mostly ladies and in any case far too old for us. Our chap wasn't anywhere near drawing his pension.'

'I wish I bloody was,' said Dover, thinking wistfully of those halcyon days whose golden hours would be unmarred by work in any shape or form. He began to grow mawkish. 'Not that I'll last that long,' he whined. 'Not with my health. I ought to be out on a disability pension now. Those damned quacks on the medical board – they've got it in for me, you know. They . . .'

'Which just leaves us with the other group, sir.' Long experience had taught MacGregor not to indulge Dover when it came to a discussion of the latter's failing powers. 'There were only seven of them, luckily. Or, at least,' he added as he recalled the insouciance with which the Holiday Ranch's books appeared to have been kept, 'that's the number the records show.'

'All men?' asked Dover, who occasionally confused everybody by not consistently being as stupid as he looked.

The question led MacGregor neatly on to the next point he wanted to make. 'Ah, that we don't know as yet, sir. The group is called the Dockwra Society and all the arrangements for the weekend they spent here were made by their secretary. We've got his name and address, but nothing about the rest of the party.'

'Can't this Major Mollie chap remember?'

'Captain Maguire, sir? I'm afraid not. He doesn't seem to take what you might call a personal interest in the people who come here.'

'Have you asked the rest of the shower that work in this dump?'

MacGregor made a point of not being caught napping as easily as that. Whilst Dover had still been sleeping it off, the sergeant had conscientiously been questioning everybody he'd met when he went in search of breakfast. 'The ones I've managed to catch so far don't seem any more helpful. The Dockwra Society only spent the weekend here – Friday evening to Sunday lunch-time. Hardly long enough to make their mark unless they did something really outrageous.'

'Like getting themselves croaked,' said Dover, indicating to MacGregor that he was ready to have the breakfast tray removed from his paunch. He began to sink once more beneath the blankets. 'Well, that's that, eh?' he murmured as he pulled the sheets up round his ears.

MacGregor viewed this development with alarm. He knew – none better – how very stressful life could become when Dover took to his bed in the middle of a murder investigation. Senior officers back at Scotland Yard just didn't understand why nothing kept on happening for weeks on end, and they were inclined to place the blame and vent their wrath on the innocent and guilty alike. 'Er – don't you think you'd better be getting dressed, sir?'

Dover uncovered one malignant, piggy eye. 'Wa'for?'

'Captain Maguire will be round in five minutes, sir.'

Dover weighed the implications carefully. Free booze was free booze and not to be sniffed at, but enough was also enough. He shook his head regretfully. 'Tell him I'm not well,' he said. 'An old war wound playing me up. Maybe I'll meet him in the bar at lunch-time.'

MacGregor suddenly realised that he might be able to find a silver lining here. 'Very well, sir,' he said carefully. 'I'll make your excuses.'

But Dover's sensitive ear had caught the nuance and he raised his head from the pillow. What was little snotty-nose up to now? 'What's he coming for?'

'Oh, only to show us round the chalets the Dockwra Society members occupied, sir,' said MacGregor nonchalantly. 'Not that there'll be anything left to see. They've all apparently been thoroughly cleaned and even occupied again since, so I doubt if there'll be much left in the way of clues. Still, I'll just pop along with Captain Maguire and have a look, shall I, sir?'

Dover shoved the bed-clothes back. 'Strewth, it was a dog's life, but he had no intention of letting a young whipper-snapper like MacGregor go stealing a march on him.

It was only then that Dover realised that he was still fully clothed.

'God damn it,' he whined as he contemplated several acres of crumpled blue serge, 'you might have taken my bloody trousers off!'

Six

'Stone a crow,' chuckled Captain Maguire ruefully, 'but we had a skinful last night! Really tied one on, eh?' Reeking pungently of the hair of the dog upon which he had breakfasted, he took a deep breath and bent down once more to his task. Which was to insert the key in the keyhole of Bunk-house Number Eleven, Shinwell Square.

Dover leaned up against the door jam. The shock of discovering that he'd slept in his best suit had been reinforced by a bracing walk, on foot, down the entire length of Barbara Castle Prospect. Captain Maguire had promised that it wasn't more than a step and would be less of an effort than getting in and out of a car. Captain Maguire had been lying in his teeth.

'Beginning to think I need glasses,' mumbled Captain Maguire as he let MacGregor take the key off him.

With Attila the Doberman Pinscher in the vanguard, they all trooped inside, out of the howling gale.

The interior of Bunk-house Number Eleven contained little of interest and less of surprise. It was exactly the same as the interior of the bunk-house in which Dover and MacGregor had spent the night. There were two bedrooms, each containing one bed which did duty either as a single or a double according to need. There was a small bathroom and an even smaller, rudimentary kitchen. All these rooms opened off a narrow corridor which ran the length of the building and into which the outside door opened. Along the front of the bunk-house ran a primitive sort of verandah equipped (if not already nicked by the neighbours) with a couple of deck chairs and a wobbly cane table. It was here that holiday-makers were expected, weather and temperature permitting, to sit well back and take their ease.

'And imbibe the odd cocktail or chota peg,' added Captain Maguire, cutting Attila off in mid-stream with a resounding thwack from his riding crop. He led the way across the sand-drifts to Bunk-house Number Twelve.

The bunk-houses which had been occupied by the Dockwra Society were grouped round three sides of Shinwell Square and formed a little, self-contained enclave. The middle of the square was taken up with a patch of coarse grass and a couple of stunted trees which Attila was not walloped for irrigating.

'We let 'em park their cars in the roadway here,' said Captain Maguire, 'as long as they don't cause an obstruction. We have a proper car park, of course, but the bastards won't use it. Insist on keeping their vehicles where they can see 'em. Not surprising, really,' he added with uncharacteristic understanding, 'when you consider the sort of clientele we get staying here.'

'Do most people come by car?' asked MacGregor, making a quick tour of the rooms in Number Twelve while Dover sat moodily on the first bed he came to.

'Fifty-fifty,' guessed Captain Maguire. 'They can get to Bowerville easily enough by train or bus, and we run 'em to and fro for a purely nominal charge.'

They moved on to Bunk-house Number Fourteen.

'No Thirteen, of course,' explained Captain Maguire, managing to find the key-hole quite quickly this time. 'Just another instance of having to capitulate to the irrational super-stitions of the labouring classes.'

'That's a master key you're using, is it, sir?' asked McGregor, mustard keen as ever to demonstrate that no detail escaped him.

54

Captain Maguire grinned. 'You could call it that, old boy,' he agreed. 'Actually, all the bloody locks are the same. Kills me to watch 'em all solemnly locking their doors when they toddle off down to the beach or wherever! Bloody peasants!'

Dover chose this moment to stick his two-pennyworth in. 'You could kick your way through these doors,' he rumbled. 'Easy as pie.'

'Too right, squire!' Captain Maguire nodded his head sadly. 'And hundreds of the beggars have done just that. Irate husbands for the most part,' he added for no apparent reason.

'I believe you said that one of the bedrooms was turned into a sort of common room, sir,' said MacGregor as they began to make yet another desultory tour of inspection.

'Yes, we moved a bed out or something. Damned imposition but we got our own back on the bill.'

'Can you remember which room it was, sir?'

Captain Maguire flicked at the sand which had drifted through onto the window sill. 'Haven't an earthly, old chum. Does it matter?'

MacGregor didn't know.

'Shall we move on then, sergeant?'

MacGregor looked round. 'Where's Chief Inspector Dover, sir?'

Captain Maguire jerked his head. 'Shot into the bog before I could warn him, old son.'

'Warn him, sir?

'You don't think we leave the water turned on in these match boxes do you, squire? Not in the middle of winter, we don't!'

Dover caught up with them as they were going through Bunk-house Number Fifteen. He gave Captain Maguire a poke in the back. 'I reckon you'd better have this,' he said, surrendering a small, chromium-plated lever. 'It sort of came off in my hand.'

With the completely fruitless inspection of the four chalets concluded, there was nothing to detain Dover and MacGregor any further at the Holiday Ranch, especially as Captain Maguire now seemed anxious to see the back of them. Indeed, his attitude had grown so unfriendly that Dover was probably right in suspecting him of not passing his hip flask round but of retiring into dark corners and taking surreptitious swigs. Dover had never been quite nippy enough to catch Captain Maguire in this inhospitable act, but the old fool wasn't a detective for nothing. He knew that honest, decent people didn't keep emerging from around corners with their eyes watering and wiping their mouths on the back of their hands.

The train had already rushed many miles southward before Dover stopped brooding on the queerness of folk in general and of Captain Maguire in particular. 'Who's this joker we're going to see now?' he asked.

By MacGregor's reckoning, this information had already been furnished three times – but who's counting? 'A man called Rupert Pettitt, sir.'

'Rupert Pettitt?' Dover tried the name for size. It didn't sound like a hard drinker. 'Who's he when he's at home?'

MacGregor appreciated that this sudden thirst for knowledge was merely a temporary aberration and unlikely to last. 'The secretary of the Dockwra Society, sir. He made all the arrangements for their weekend at the Holiday Ranch.'

'That was a funny sort of place,' said Dover reflectively. 'You wouldn't catch me spending my bloody leave in a dump like that. The wife's always saying we ought to try one of these holiday camp places but I've always put my foot down.' Even to those not privileged to have made Mrs Dover's acquaintance this male chauvinist boast would have sounded unconvincing. 'Expecting us, is he?'

'Rupert Pettitt, sir? No, he's not, actually.' MacGregor was on a hiding to nothing, and he knew it. Whichever way he responded to Dover's question, he was laying himself open to the old fool's nit-picking.

Dover didn't disappoint him. 'You damned fool, suppose he's not in? If I go traipsing all the way across London to Wapping and then find . . .'

'It's Hither Green, actually, sir.'

'Same thing!' snarled Dover. He scowled. 'Now you've made me forget what I was bloody saying!'

'I didn't want to warn him, sir. Forewarned is forearmed, you know.'

'You reckon this joker's a wrong 'un?' Dover was ever on the look-out for a speedy and spectacular conclusion.

'I don't know anything about him at all, sir. He may even have no connection with the case. It's simply that I'd sooner not give him the chance to cook up some story or other before we can get at him.'

'Cook up some story?' parroted Dover, who knew what he was talking about. 'You want to watch it, laddie. They call that sort of talk "police harrassment" these days.'

'I'm only going to ask a few perfectly straightforward questions, sir.'

'Then why,' demanded Dover in a squawk of vulgar triumph as MacGregor neatly entered the trap and closed the door behind him, 'didn't you warn him we were coming? Take it from me, laddie, if I've been dragged all the way out to Kempton Park on a bloody wild goose chase, you'll not live long enough to regret it!'

MacGregor sighed and got his cigarettes out. They were in a non-smoking compartment but what the hell if it put a gag in Dover's mouth for a bit.

If Hither Green can be said to have a Caribbean Quarter, Mr Pettitt lived slap-bang in the middle of it. He occupied a largish, three-storied house – the only one in the entire terrace which, if the absence of a bank of doorbells was anything to go by, hadn't been turned into flats. This apparent anomaly was explained by the fact that Mr Pettitt used part of his house for his business.

'A chiropodist?' said Dover when he'd limped his way from the taxi across the pavement. Mr Pettitt's profession was proclaimed only very modestly on a small brass plate, but Dover's failing eyesight rarely missed anything which might be turned to his advantage. He fancied that he could improve this shining hour and snatched MacGregor's hand away from the bell.

'Hang on a minute! We haven't worked out how we're going to play this one.'

MacGregor bit his lip. Dear God, it was like running in double harness with a reject from the *Boy's Own Paper*! 'Oh, I think we "play it" perfectly straight, sir. I'll just tell him who we are and . . .'

Dover was still hanging onto MacGregor's arm. Well, it was marginally better than taking the whole weight on his own aching feet. 'I've had a better idea,' he hissed. 'Let's pretend I'm a patient. Then, while he's having a dekko at this corn of mine, we can sort of manoeuvre the conversation round to holiday camps and then' – even Dover's imagination occasionally had its limits – 'play it by ear.'

MacGregor shook his head and, detaching Dover's fingers, rang the bell. 'I don't think so, sir,' he said. 'That kind of duplicity tends to give the police a bad name. After all, we aren't undercover agents, are we? We're simply going to ask for information and assistance from a respectable, law-abiding citizen.'

'Says who?' demanded Dover who believed everybody guilty until proved innocent, and sometimes even afterwards. He was infuriated that his plan had been rejected and was determined that somebody should pay for it. It could be MacGregor or it could be this blooming toe-doctor – at the moment he didn't care much which.

A woman in a white coat answered the door and conducted the two detectives into an empty waiting room. After the statutory delay of three or four minutes, another door opened and Mr Pettitt himself invited them into his surgery.

In spite of the chiropodist's efforts to direct him elsewhere Dover made a bee-line for the treatment chair and heaved himself into it. MacGregor found a seat at a table and cleared a space for his notebook amongst the jumble of sharp-bladed instruments, packets of lamb's wool and reels of sticking plaster.

This left Mr Pettitt standing forlornly in the middle of his own surgery but eventually he pulled himself together and sat down on a small white stool. Since this was where he habitually sat when he was working, it was near the treatment chair. Dover rattled a heavy boot like a mendicant friar shaking his begging bowl.

Mr Pettitt wiped the palms of his hands down the front of his white coat and peered up at Dover through pebble-thick glasses.

'No point in sitting there doing nothing,' said Dover with every appearance of reasonableness. 'Left foot, little toe.'

Mr Pettitt, two of whom would hardly have furnished even a Continental breakfast for Dover, failed to tell the great man exactly where he could stick his left foot. He contented himself with a discontented pout and, bending down, began to fiddle with the laces on Dover's boot.

MacGregor opened the interrogation. 'I believe you are the secretary of the Dockwra Society, sir?'

The little chiropodist paused in his struggle with the knots in Dover's laces. 'Honorary secretary,' he corrected in a light, precise voice.

'I wonder if you could tell us, sir, what precisely this Dockwra Society is.'

Mr Pettitt took his time. He got the laces untied and, removing Dover's boot, placed it neatly on the floor before replying. 'Why do you wish to know?'

'We think it might help us with our enquiries, sir.'

Unperturbed by the large holes and the acrid pong, Mr Pettitt slowly removed Dover's sock and tucked it into the boot for safe-keeping. 'What enquiries are those, sergeant?'

MacGregor frowned. Like most policemen, he equated uncooperativeness with guilt, and there was no doubt that this four-eyed, bald-headed little squirt was definitely being uncooperativ 'I'm afraid I'm not at liberty to reveal details at this moment, sir, but we are currently engaged on a matter of some importance.' MacGregor paused before issuing the threat that generally brought them to heel. 'Of course, if you'd rather continue the conversation down at the police station, sir . . .'

Mr Pettitt removed his glasses, huffed on them and polished them on his handkerchief before replacing them on his nose.

'The Dockwra Society is a small group of stamp collectors. It is named after a very early pioneer of the penny post.'

Dover waved his bare foot in the air. 'On the little toe!'

Mr Pettitt leaned forward to make a closer examination and then started to rummage amongst the surgical-looking instruments which MacGregor had displaced on the table.

Dover eyed the scalpel with some anxiety. 'Hey, watch it!' he advised. 'It's as tender as hell.'

'It's only a corn,' said Mr Pettitt mildly. 'It looks as though somebody's been hacking at it with a razor blade.'

'That was the wife,' said Dover, one of nature's rats. 'I told her not to.'

'It's a highly inadvisable proceeding, whoever is responsible.'

'Somebody had to do something,' retorted Dover. 'It was throbbing fit to bust. They don't give you sick leave in the police for a bad toe, you know.'

Mr Pettitt didn't appear to be listening. He was no stranger to the results of DIY chiropody. When he got round to opening his mouth again, his remarks were addressed to MacGregor. 'We began the Dockwra Society a couple of years ago. It's very small and informal. We specialise in pre-war European issues.'

'EEEEEyouch!' howled Dover, lashing out with the foot that wasn't clamped between Mr Pettitt's knees. 'That bloody hurt, you sadist!'

'You've really only yourself to blame,' murmured Mr Pettitt, pushing his spectacles back up his nose. 'If you had consulted a qualified practitioner and . . .'

'Would you mind telling me how many members you've got, sir?'

'About twenty. We're hoping to attract more in time.'

'You had a meeting of some sort at the Rankin's Holiday Ranch at Bowerville-by-the-sea, I believe.'

'That is correct. It was our annual general meeting. We picked a location which was as central as possible.'

'Bloody hell!' screamed Dover. 'Mind what you're doing!'

Mr Pettitt reached for the cotton wool. 'We'll have to leave it for a few days for the inflammation to go down. Come back next week.'

'You've a hope!' snarled Dover, who didn't suffer sadists gladly. 'What the hell's that?'

'Just a piece of sticking plaster to keep the wound clean.'

Dover's eyes narrowed. 'When I came in here, mate,' he snarled, 'I didn't have a wound!' He watched Mr Pettitt pick his boot and sock up. 'You got a list of the morons who were at this crummy meeting of yours?'

Mr Pettitt blinked. 'Yes.'

'Let's be having it, then!'

'What do you want it for?'

Dover was blowed if he could remember. He fell back on MacGregor again. 'Got a fag, laddie?'

Mr Pettitt courageously scotched that idea. 'I'm afraid I don't permit smoking anywhere on the premises. I'm allergic to tobacco smoke.'

'I'll bet you're a bloody tee-totaller, too!' said Dover, really stripping the kid gloves off.

Mr Pettitt turned back to MacGregor. 'You were asking about our meeting at Bowerville-by-the-sea?'

'We're looking for a middle-aged man, sir,' said MacGregor, feeling that the least he could do was put his cards on the table. 'About five-foot eight. False teeth. Dark hair. Plumpish. Would that description fit one of your members, sir?'

'It might,' said Mr Pettitt cautiously. 'What's he done?'

McGregor took out the photograph which had been taken in situ on the Muncaster rubbish tip and passed it across. 'Not very nice, I'm afraid, sir, but can you recognise him?'

Mr Pettitt shook his head.

'But the description would fit one of your members?'

Mr Pettitt gestured at the photograph with his free hand. 'You're not suggesting that this . . .'

'It's a strong possibility, sir. Now, there were seven of you all told at the Holiday Ranch, I believe? If we could just go through them and if you could let me have their names and addresses at the same time . . .'

Mr Pettitt had to fetch the relevant papers from his private quarters but he was back in the surgery before Dover had found anything worth pocketing. 'Well, let's get the people who definitely can't be the person in your snapshot out of the way first, shall we, sergeant? There's me, of couse.' Mr Pettitt's lips parted in a death's head grin. 'I am obviously not the dead man. Nor, I imagine, is Mrs Hall. Mrs Norah Hall.'

'You have lady members, then?' asked MacGregor as he took down the address.

'Only the one,' said Mr Pettitt. 'But she's most keen and very knowledgeable, especially about French colonials.'

'And the next, sir?'

'I don't think it can be young Keith Osmond,' Mr Pettitt went on thoughfully. 'He's a tall, big-boned chap in his late twenties so he doesn't fit at all. Nor, I fancy, does Mr Michael Ruscoe. He's middle-aged, I suppose, but he's rather small and wiry.'

'Could I have the addresses, sir?'

Mr Pettitt read out the information at dictation speed and obligingly spelt out any proper names he thought might cause difficulty.

MacGregor did his mental arithmetic. 'That leaves three more.'

'Mr Braithwaite would be too old, I imagine. He must be nearly sixty. He has a beard, too.'

'We're pretty certain our chap was clean shaven, sir.'

'Then there's Gordon Valentine, but I had a letter from him only this morning.'

'That would seem to eliminate him, sir,' agreed MacGregor, 'but I'll still need to take down his particulars, if you don't mind.'

Mr Pettitt remained silent for several moments after Mac-Gregor's pen stopped moving over the page. 'That leaves us with Mr Knapper, sergeant,' he said at last. 'Mr George Arthur Knapper. He, I am very much afraid, might well fit your bill.'

Seven

'He was a bloody cold fish,' grumbled Dover in whom the milk of human kindness had curdled beyond recall. 'Callous.'

'He did explain that he'd never actually met any of them before, sir.' MacGregor was not unaware that the tendency to contradict everything Dover said was becoming a reflex action. 'They weren't personal friends and he claims to have hardly exchanged more than half-a-dozen words with Knapper.'

'Shifty-looking devil, too,' muttered Dover. 'Got a touch of the Crippen about him. Sadistic.' He contemplated his left foot which was propped up on a convenient chair. 'I'll lay you odds he did it.'

It was not unusual for Dover to make these premature judgements about people to whom he had taken a dislike. Most of his cases were littered with suspects upon whom he had pinned guilt or innocence in much the same spirit as blindfolded children pin the tail on the donkey. MacGregor wasn't, therefore, unduly worried when Dover pointed the grubby finger of accusation at Mr Pettitt. If previous experience was anything to go by he would only be the first of a dozen before the chief inspector lost all interest and threw in the towel.

Our two heroes had retired to a nearby hostelry to discuss these latest developments. Since they were in London, it might have been expected that they would have repaired to their office in Scotland Yard but, at that particular moment in time, Dover was somewhat persona non grata with his colleagues. One would have thought that, after all these years, they'd have got used to having him hanging around – dandruff, constipation, dyspepsia, foot rot and all – but they hadn't. Some hot-tempered spirits had been so carried away by their professional pride that they'd even threatened to boot Dover from one end of Victoria Street to the other if he showed his face round the Murder Squad again. It would all blow over in time, of course. Old Bailey judges are always making scathing remarks about the criminal incompetence of the police.

'Actually, sir,' said MacGregor, steeling himself to look on the bright side, 'I think we're beginning to make a little progress.'

Dover sank his face into his beer. 'Ugh.'

'Our next move is obviously to investigate this Knapper man.'

'Ugh, ugh.'

'It's a pity, though,' MacGregor continued grimly in the face of considerable discouragement, 'that Mr Pettitt couldn't provide us with a bit more information. Still, we've got enough to make a start.'

'Lying in his teeth!' proclaimed Dover, emerging from his tankard with a gratified belch. 'I wouldn't believe a word that butcher said even if it was true. 'Strewth, did you see the way he drove that spike thing into me? And enjoyed doing it!'

MacGregor was checking assiduously through his notes. This was partly because he was a conscientious detective and partly because it was getting to the end of the month and he didn't want to have to notice that Dover's glass was empty. 'Mr Pettitt says he saw Knapper alive and well on the Sunday morning, sir. The Dockwra Society finished off their meeting before lunch on Sunday and most people, including Pettitt himself and Knapper, left almost immediately. Pettitt had a car but he thinks Knapper was travelling by train.' MacGregor frowned and glanced up. Occasionally it was convenient to take advantage of the fact that Dover was as thick as two planks to bounce a few ideas off him. 'That's rather odd, isn't it, sir?'

Dover chose to be facetious. 'Millions of people travel by train, laddie! Every day.'

'I mean, odd that ·Mr Pettitt didn't offer Knapper a lift, sir. They both live in London.'

'Return ticket,' grunted Dover.

'You can easily get a refund, sir.'

'Maybe Pettitt couldn't stand the sight of him.'

'I still think it's rather odd, sir.'

Dover was now intent on scraping noisy figures-of-eight on the table with his tankard. 'He could have offered,' he pointed out impatiently, 'and it was Knapper who said no.'

'Meaning that he wasn't returning home directly to London after the weekend at Bowerville, sir?' MacGregor seized eagerly on the idea. 'Yes, that's a very interesting speculation. I must get onto the Holiday Ranch and see if they can remember if they provided Knapper with transport to the station.'

Dover could see that the subtle approach wasn't getting him anywhere. 'Got a fag, laddie?' he asked. He waited until MacGregor had got his cigarettes and lighter out before delivering the coup de grâce. 'And I'll have a refill, too, while you're at it.'

There was something of a hiatus before they got Dover back in the rhythm of dragging cigarette smoke into his lungs and pouring best bitter down his gullet. When all was sweetness and light once more, MacGregor broached a new topic of conversation: matrimony.

'I suppose Mr Knapper must be a bachelor, sir. Or, at least, not living with his wife.'

'Why?'

'A wife would surely have reported her husband's disappearance to the authorities by now, wouldn't she, sir?'

The beer must be having a mellowing effect. 'Like a shot!' agreed Dover. 'Any threat to their meal ticket and you can't see 'em for dust. Like leeches,' he added with the grim resignation of one who was required to hand over his pay cheque intact

65

every month. He made an effort and switched his mind to happier themes. 'Did that foot chap say anything about any rows or punch-ups on this blooming weekend?'

MacGregor could only assume that it had been anxiety about his corn that had stopped Dover from listening to what Mr Pettitt had said. 'No, it all seems to have been very amicable, sir. Actually, there hardly seems to have been time for any violent passions to develop, especially as nobody had ever met anybody before. They didn't arrive at the Holiday Ranch until the Friday evening and, by the time they'd got settled in, had a meal and a drink or two, it was time for bed. They started having their meeting or whatever it was at ten o'clock on the Saturday, broke off for the venison lunch, and then carried on till six. They had a cold supper, another drink or so and off to bed again. On Sunday morning they had a brief meeting after breakfast just to tie up a few loose ends, and that was that. They cleared off home as and when it suited them.'

"Strewth!' said Dover whose own life, while hardly exciting, was more fun-packed than that.

MacGregor was making a note in his notebook. 'I must get on to the local police and see if they can find out what train Knapper caught from Bowerville-by-the-sea.'

'You could check if he got a train to Muncaster,' rumbled Dover, apparently enjoying one of his more inspired moments.

'I'll check all the trains out of Bowerville that Sunday morning, sir,' promised MacGregor, 'wherever they were going. And I'll check the buses, too.'

Dover waited until he'd got both hands clasped round his third pint before uttering again. 'Have you seen the gents' toilet in your travels, laddie?'

It was a tedious journey out to the suburb where Mr Knapper had had – and perhaps still did have – his residence, but Dover stood it well. Thanks to his bad toe, which was giving him more gyp now than before Mr Pettitt had got his murderous hands on it, they'd gone the whole way by taxi and MacGregor had passed the time wondering miserably how on earth he was going to fiddle this on his expenses sheet.

Number one hundred and seventy-six (or 'Doreenland') was, architecturally speaking, identical with all the other two hundred and four houses in the road but a gallant fight for individuality was being waged by the people who lived there. Number one hundred and seventy-six had not lagged behind in the drive to be different. No other house in the road (and probably not in the whole of North London) could boast a yellow front door and shutters plus a triangular goldfish pond under the bay window.

MacGregor opened the simulated wrought-iron garden gate and led the way up the crazy paving. He rang the door chimes.

Dover gave it a generous thirty seconds. 'Nobody at home!' he announced gratefully and prepared to waddle back down the path.

Unluckily for him, the door opened. MacGregor raised his hat and politely asked the obvious question.

'Who wants to know?'

Carefully MacGregor explained that they were detectives from Scotland Yard engaged in making some enquiries. Carefully the lady who'd answered the door read through both warrant cards from first to last whilst Dover huffed and puffed with impatience on her doorstep.

'I'm Mrs Knapper,' admitted Mrs Knapper at last, and dared either man to take advantage of the fact. She was a woman who just missed being attractive. The eyes were a little too shrewd, the jaw a little too square, the arms a little too muscular.

MacGregor flashed his dimples nonetheless. 'Actually,' he said, 'It's really *Mr* Knapper we'd like to have a word with.'

'He's not here.'

Dover got a boot in before the door closed.

Mrs Knapper's face hardened. 'Watch it, fattie!' she advised. 'One scratch on that paintwork and I'll have you for wilful and malicious damage!'

'I wonder if you can tell us where we can get in touch with

Mr Knapper?' asked MacGregor, recklessly interposing his body between the point of Mrs Knapper's chin and Dover's fist. Not that the chief inspector would really have struck a defenceless woman, of course. Not in front of witnesses he wouldn't.

'No, I can't.'

The curtain twitching in the windows of the houses on either side was growing phrenetic while further down the street doorstep sweeping and cat-summoning was reaching epidemic proportions.

MacGregor leaned forward. 'Do you think we might perhaps step inside for just a moment, madam? I'm sure you don't want all your neighbours . . .'

'Stuff the neighbours!' said Mrs Knapper, stepping forward to deliver a two-fingered salute up and down the road. 'Mr Knapper's scarpered,' she said when she'd time to be bothered with the matter in hand again. 'Done a bunk! Deserted me. And good riddance to bad rubbish, if you ask me. For all the good he was I might as well have taken my old grannie to bed with me.'

The problem of Dover's growing impatience went clean out of MacGregor's mind. 'Mr Knapper's gone? When?'

Mrs Knapper was not without a certain rude sense of humour. 'Well, parts of him went years ago, if you must know, but he finally pushed off for good and all a couple of months ago.' Her temporary good natured mood vanished as a dreadful thought struck her. 'Here, don't tell me you stupid bastards have gone and found the dirty-minded little bleeder?'

Understandably MacGregor hesitated.

'Well, he's not coming back here!' snapped Mrs Knapper in a voice that brooked no argument. 'I've had enough of him and his nasty habits to last me a bloody life-time. If you want that sort of thing, I told him straight, you effing well go and pay for it. There's some as don't mind what they do for money but I'm not one of 'em.'

There might have been some even more dramatic revelations if Mrs Knapper's spate had not been interrupted by a bellow from the back of the house. 'Doreen!' came a deep, masculine voice.

Without turning her head Mrs Knapper bawled back. 'What?'

'Get your skates on, for Christ's sake! You seen the time?'

'I'm just coming!'

Since Mrs Knapper didn't appear to be going to offer any explanation of this exchange, MacGregor pressed on with his questions about her errant husband. 'Could you tell me what happened exactly?'

'Nothing happened!' retorted Mrs Knapper. 'He just cleared off one weekend and never come back. No explanation and no effing letter left on the mantelpiece.'

'What about his things?'

Mrs Knapper stiffened. 'What about 'em?'

'Did he take all his belongings or did he leave some of them behind?'

'I gave him a fortnight,' said Mrs Knapper, slightly on the defensive, 'and then I flogged the lot. Clothes, books, bloody stamps, everything. I needed the room. Besides,' – she folded her arms – 'he told me to.'

'He told you to?' repeated MacGregor.

'Years ago. When we were first married. "If anything happens to me, Doreen," he said, "you destroy everything. Don't hang about! Burn all my papers and get rid of the rest." So I did.'

'What did he say that for?'

'How do I know?' Mrs Knapper was beginning to get as fed up with all this doorstep interrogation as Dover was. 'Probably trying to make himself look all romantic and mysterious. Like a spy or something. He was for ever playing silly buggers like that. I stopped paying him any attention years ago.'

Dover lowered himself gingerly onto the little party wall which separated the Knapper front garden from its neighbour. He'd been pondering on the move for some time and had finally reached the conclusion that, while his poor feet were a present reality, piles were only a future possibility.

MacGregor hurried on. 'You say your husband went off one weekend? Have you any idea where he was going?'

'If he said, I wasn't listening. He was alway buzzing off some place or other.'

'Did he ever mention Rankin's Holiday Ranches? Or Bowerville-by-the-sea? Or Muncaster?

As far as the gutter press was concerned, Mrs Knapper was a well-read woman. 'That stiff they found on the rubbish heap?' she asked with considerable interest. 'You think that's Arthur?'

MacGregor admitted that this possibility had indeed crossed the police mind. He repeated the official description of the body.

Mrs Knapper had no doubts. 'That's him!' she declared roundly. 'Here, haven't you got a picture or something?'

MacGregor reluctantly produced his gruesome photograph.

'Cor strike a light!' Even Mrs Knapper was taken aback. 'Blimey,' she said, 'they give him a right going over, didn't they? Still,' – she recovered her natural optimism and handed the photograph back to MacGregor – 'it's him. I'll take my Bible oath on it.'

'Had your husband any identifying marks on his body?'

'Smooth as a baby's bottom!' said Mrs Knapper cheerfully. 'Just like a fat, white slug. Here,' – her eyes sparkled – 'there'll be compensation for this, won't there? Beside the insurance, I mean. Well, he's been the victim of criminal violence, he has, and we were man and wife. I'm his bleeding next of kin and everything.' She ran her tongue over her lips. 'I wonder if the Citizen's Advice is still open? Oh, well,' – she relaxed and propped herself up comfortably against the door jamb – 'there's no hurry, is there? First thing tomorrow morning'll do.'

Approaching footsteps came heavily down the hall and the figure of a man loomed up behind Mrs Knapper's shoulder. He was a big man with an unshaven chin and a sweaty check shirt sagging seductively open to the navel.

'What you doing, Doreen?' he demanded.

Mrs Knapper turned her head to smile at the newcomer with a smug, proprietary smile. 'Shan't be just a sec, George,' she cooed. 'It's only the fuzz. You go and get yourself another beer or something, love.'

'The fuzz? What the hell do they want?'

'They've come about Arthur.'

'That little sod!'

'He's dead, love,' said Mrs Knapper in the mildest of mild reproof.

'Not before bleeding time!' growled George and withdrew from the scene.

Mrs Knapper smiled indulgently after him and, this time, vouchsafed an explanation. 'He's my lodger. He's a lovely man but he can't bear being kept waiting, if you follow my meaning.'

MacGregor preferred not to. 'When did you last see your husband?'

'A couple of months ago, I suppose. I forget.'

'And you say he often went away from home?'

'Sometimes.' Mrs Knapper shrugged her shoulders in eloquent indifference. 'To tell you the truth, it got so's I hardly noticed. He'd got his hobbies and I'd' – she jerked her head ever so slightly in the direction of the absent George – 'I'd got mine.'

MacGregor watched rather hopelessly as Mrs Knapper took a packet of cigarettes out of her pocket and flicked her lighter. It was a spectacle calculated to have Dover running amuck. 'Why didn't you report Mr Knapper's disappearance to the police?' asked MacGregor as he assiduously gave Dover his own nicotine comforter.

'How was I to know he'd snuffed it? I thought he'd just taken a powder or something. And what with him being so secretive and everything, I reckoned the last thing he wanted was publicity.'

'But what about his work?'

'What about it?'

'Didn't anybody come round making enquiries when he didn't show up?'

'Piano tuner,' said Mrs Knapper shortly. 'Self-employed.

One or two of 'em did ring up to ask where the hell he'd got to so I just said he was poorly and he'd be getting in touch.'

Even a cigarette wasn't going to hold Dover much longer. MacGregor broke into a gabble. 'Is there anything left that might have Mr Knapper's fingerprints on it?'

'So's you can compare 'em with the corpse's?' Mrs Knapper shook her head. 'I don't think so. I made a clean sweep, you see, while I was at it. Still' – she flipped her lighted cigarette end, neatly and accurately, into her next-door neighbour's front garden – 'you don't have to bother about things like that. I'll identify him for you. No trouble.'

There were numerous other questions that MacGregor felt he ought to ask but Dover was already thinking about clambering to his feet. MacGregor accepted the inevitable and politely raised his hat. 'Very well, madam,' he said, 'I'll make all the necessary arrangements. I'm afraid we shall have to ask you to go up to Muncaster to make the identification and give evidence at the inquest.'

'Just as long as I get my expenses,' said Mrs Knapper comfortably.

MacGregor felt that, in the interest of justice, he ought to issue a warning. 'You do realise that you mustn't say the dead man is your husband unless you're absolutely sure? It's a criminal offence to . . .'

But Mrs Knapper was lending both ears to another raucous bellow from the back of the house. George was getting restless again. 'I'll be sure, dear,' she promised MacGregor with a vague but kindly smile. Although nothing like the man George was, the sergeant was quite a handsome, well-set-up young fellow . . . and you never knew. 'I mean, even if the face's gone, the *body*'s still there, isn't it? I'll recognise that all right, or bits of it.'

Dover began tottering back painfully down the garden path and MacGregor fired off yet another question before Mrs Knapper was lost to him, perhaps for ever. 'Had your husband any enemies?'

'He was his own worst, dear. I was always telling him that.'

'Had he any friends or acquaintances who might be able to help us with our enquiries?'

Mrs Knapper's reply came through the rapidly narrowing crack in the door. 'He kept himself very much to himself.'

'You don't know of anyone who . . .?'

'Sorry, dear!'

It was a good thirty-six hours before the next development of any importance took place in the great Muncaster Municipal Dump Murder Mystery, the mills of God having very little on Chief Inspector Dover when it came to a slow grind.

Eight

Not that everything came to a standstill, of course. There was the usual mountain of paperwork to be completed and the activities of a large team of investigators to be coordinated. The backroom boys needed supervision and then there was the mass of complicated travel arrangements which had to be put in hand in order to get Mrs Knapper up to the mortuary in Muncaster to see if the dead man was her husband.

While all these chores fell to MacGregor's lot, it mustn't be thought that Chief Inspector Dover sat there for a day and a half just twiddling his thumbs. Far from it. Each hour of Dover's time was so action-packed with eating and sleeping that he'd practically no time left over for thumb-twiddling at all.

By late afternoon on the day after their encounter with Mrs Knapper, MacGregor began to feel that things were moving at last. He received a telephone call from one of his opposite numbers in Muncaster to the effect that Mrs Knapper had identified the body from the rubbish dump as Mr Knapper. So positive was she that she had, in fact, made the identification even before the mortuary attendant had raised the corner of the sheet from the corpse's face. It had apparently been a very emotional business, with Mrs Knapper weeping hysterically and vowing to sue her husband's murderer for every penny he possessed.

'Sue him?' asked MacGregor, mildly intrigued. 'On what grounds?'

'Would you believe alienation of affections?' asked the man in Muncaster. 'She reckons that whoever croaked her old man deprived her of her marital rights.' He chuckled at the joke.

'She'd probably win,' said MacGregor who'd grown very cynical over the years. 'It wouldn't be any dafter than some of the things the courts have been doing recently. Still,' – he returned conscientiously to the matter in hand – 'she made a positive identification, you say? Well, it shouldn't be too difficult to confirm that, now we know where to look.'

'By the way,' said the Muncaster man, who enjoyed a chat when he wasn't paying for the call, 'she said something that might be significant when we were having a cup of tea together afterwards.'

'Oh?'

'I was sort of twitting her about not reporting it when her old man went missing and she said he'd had a premonition that something was going to happen to him.'

MacGregor cocked an ear. 'She mentioned something like that when I spoke to her.'

'If you ask me, she's probably making the whole thing up but she claims he warned her months ago that he was involved in something dangerous and that he might have to make a run for it and go into hiding at a moment's notice.'

'You know the man was a piano tuner!'

'Well, that's as maybe, but Mrs K was quite adamant that he was afraid he might have to drop out of circulation all of a sudden and, if he did, she was to keep her trap shut about it. No tattling to the cops or the neighbours or anybody.'

Down in London MacGregor shook his head doubtfully. 'Forget it,' he said. 'All she's doing is trying to cover up for what she actually did – which was damn all. The truth is that the lodger moved in as soon as the husband was out of sight, if not before – and she flogged all old Knapper's personal belongings for what she could get for 'em.'

'Well, I'm just giving you her version,' said the man in Muncaster easily. 'And warning you that she'll stick to it. I reckon she's getting ready to answer a few awkward questions from the coroner.'

MacGregor couldn't resist the temptation to probe a little further. 'Did she say that Knapper was worried about being killed?'

The telephone wires crackled gently. 'No, I don't think she did exactly. More that he might have to disappear suddenly – whatever that means.'

'She didn't ask?'

'Not her. Too chuffed at seeing the back of the poor sod, or hoping to, rather. That's always assuming, of course, that there's a word of truth in her story – which I doubt.'

As soon as MacGregor had expressed his fulsome gratitude for all the whole-hearted cooperation he had received from the stout-hearted lads up there in good old Muncaster, he put the phone down and, almost immediately, picked it up again. He had to try and organise some further proof that their dead man really was Arthur Knapper. In spite of Mrs Knapper's alleged spring cleaning, MacGregor still thought it worth expending a few man-hours in giving the Knapper matrimonial home a good going over. Anything – a hair, a fingerprint, an old toothbrush – could well prove invaluable in bolstering up the widow's somewhat facile evidence. Then Knapper's doctor and his dentist had to be contacted to see if they could help, and there were several more avenues that could be explored should these initial efforts come to naught. It was always easier, MacGregor reflected ruefully, to find what you were looking for when you knew where it was.

Actually, though, MacGregor had few doubts that it was Arthur George Knapper, piano tuner and stamp collector, and he began to work out his next steps on that basis. Clearly, all the people who had been with Knapper on that weekend at the Holiday Ranch at Bowerville-by-the-sea would now have to be interviewed as a matter of urgency. Even Dover would appreciate that. The order in which these potential suspects –

because that's what they probably were — were going to be seen needed sorting out, though. It was a nuisance that they seemed to be scattered all over the country. MacGregor got out a large-scale map of England and Wales and spread it out over his desk and began, with the help of the list of addresses extracted from Mr Pettitt, to work out his itinerary.

Mrs Nora Hall drew the number one spot on the agenda and it was the garden gate leading to her cottage that MacGregor dragged open for Dover on the following morning.

Dover, the embodiment of suburban blight, didn't have much feeling for the country life. ''Strewth,' he ejaculated as he picked his way gingerly up a chaotic little garden path bordered with beds of rotting cabbages and mouldering sprouts, 'what a pong!'

MacGregor didn't lightly agree with any sentiment expressed by Dover but, on this occasion, he had to admit that the old fool had hit the nail on the head. What with the shortcomings of rural sanitation and an obsessive devotion to fertilisers, the atmosphere surrounding Mrs Hall's ramshackle cottage did come rather thick and strong.

MacGregor knocked on the front door and was immediately savaged by a rambling rose. 'We're probably expected to go round the back, sir,' he said to Dover when he'd stopped the bleeding.

They both gazed disconsolately at the small lake of mud which lay between them and the rear of the cottage.

'See if the door's locked!' urged Dover. 'They never lock their doors in the country.'

Not true.

'Bloody hell!' said Dover.

MacGregor tried to peer through the windows but they were too well guarded with coarse lace curtains and dirt. He sighed, wished he wasn't wearing his posh Italian shoes and offered Dover his arm. Not that he wouldn't have been in ecstasy if Dover had fallen flat on his face in the slurry but he had learned not to be self-indulgent in these matters.

Moving slowly from one half-submerged stepping stone to another, the two detectives rounded the corner of the cottage only to find their way barred by parts of an old iron bedstead, behind which a half-grown billy goat waited hopefully for them with a dark, malicious little face.

Dover and MacGregor backed off. They would, indeed, have made a strategic withdrawal if it had not been for a gaggle of geese which moved in, hissing angrily, behind them.

Dover, although unaccustomed to making such value judgements, tried to work out where the main threat lay. As soon as he had got this straight, he intended to manoeuvre Mac-Gregor's unblemished young body into the front line.

Luckily, rescue was at hand and Dover was not called upon to make the supreme sacrifice of somebody else. A strange, bulky figure carrying a bucket emerged from one of the outbuildings. It was a woman and, taking in the situation at a glance, she came sloshing across through the mud and the muck, scattering a flock of bantams in all directions.

'You must be the chappies from Scotland Yard!' she bellowed, sending the billy goat on its way with a good-natured gum-boot up the backside. As her be-mittened fingers fumbled awkwardly with the binder twine and electric flex which held the iron bedstead shut, she turned and called back over her shoulder, 'They're here, Mavis!' She manhandled the bedstead out of the way and addressed herself to Dover. 'I'm Nora Hall,' she said. 'Wouldn't you feel more comfortable inside?' She discouraged the geese from accepting the invitation by biffing them affectionately round the ears with her bucket.

Dover and MacGregor, watching *very* carefully where they put their feet, went round to the back door and into the tiny kitchen.

Mrs Hall kicked off her gum boots and cleared a space on the table for her bucket. 'Sorry about the imbroglio but we've had one hell of a morning with the old sow.'

MacGregor eyed the kitchen table with dismay. Bits of food fought for lebensraum with unwashed crockery, grubby towels were draped higgledy-piggledy over blackened saucepans and a dishcloth lay forlornly across a thick brown liquid. In the middle of everything crouched a large ginger cat which interrupted its assiduous licking of a piece of butter paper only to glare at the intruders.

'Come through into the parlour!' invited Mrs Hall, conducting Dover and MacGregor into an even smaller room but which at least had the virtue, since it was never used, of being tidier.

Dover sank thankfully into an easy chair by the empty fireplace, and then wondered if he'd done the right thing. If he'd been worried about getting piles from the stone wall outside Mrs Knapper's front door, what were his emotions as he sank into cushions so cold and clammy that you could have grown watercress on them? Dover tugged his overcoat more closely over his paunch, screwed his bowler hat further down his forehead, and miserably hoped for the bloody best.

MacGregor had naturally been taking a less subjective interest in his surroundings. He noted the musty, unlived-in atmosphere of the room, of course, but his attention was chiefly drawn to an overly large Victorian sideboard in a bellicose mahogany which stood against one wall. On the sideboard was evidence of Mrs Hall's little hobby – a brand new Stanley Gibbon's stamp catalogue, a stamp album, a packet of stamp hinges and a pair of tweezers.

MacGregor was just about to get things under way by some friendly query about the attractions of philately when the hitherto unseen Mavis came padding in on stockinged feet.

'Oh, please don't get up!' she cooed, to Dover's complete bewilderment. 'I don't want to interrupt.' She slid self-effacingly onto a stool by the door.

'My associate, Mavis Beauvis,' said Mrs Hall gruffly. 'We breed pedigree goats together.' She indicated her two visitors with a hand which bore much evidence of honest toil. 'And these are the chaps from Scotland Yard, dear! That one's Detective Chief Inspector Dover and this is Detective Sergeant MacGregor.' Mrs Hall, having taken a good hard look at Dover, very sensibly directed all her subsequent remarks to MacGregor. 'You don't mind if Mavis stays, do you? Just as a chaperone.'

MacGregor shook his head though privately he thought Mrs Hall could well have cooled the ardour of even the randiest male with one hand tied behind her back. Still, if she wanted a chaperone, she could have one. There were other aspects of her personality that he was finding much more puzzling. Like – was the woman psychic or something.

Mrs Hall cleared her throat. She was a busy woman and pedigree goats wait for no man. 'Fire away, sergeant!'

MacGregor fired and the outcome was, information-wise, a lemon. Mrs Hall, astounding in her ability to answer questions almost before they were asked, had little to tell and nothing that Dover and MacGregor didn't already know.

Mrs Hall was a keen member of the Dockwra Society and when the Annual General Meeting at Rankin's Holiday Ranch had been announced had thought she might as well toddle along. 'I felt I needed the break,' she explained. 'You can stomach just so much of pedigree goats, you know, and old Mavis here kindly volunteered to hold the fort while I took a couple of days off.'

Old Mavis smirked demurely. 'I do feel it's important that we don't live in each other's pockets the whole time,' she simpered.

'Oh, quite,' said MacGregor. 'Now, was Mr Knapper already there when you arrived at the Holiday Ranch?'

Mrs Hall nodded. 'I was tail-end Charlie, if I remember correctly. Spot of muck in the carburettor, you know, and had to stop off at a garage to borrow their air-line to clear it.'

'And you were allocated a bedroom in Bunkhouse number .. ?'

'Twelve. That was the hut we had our room for meetings in so, at night, I had the place to myself. I was the only female present, you see. It was jolly thoughtful of Mr Pettitt,' she added seriously, 'and I appreciate it. I've always been the sort of lass who likes to see the proprieties observed.'

'Oh, quite,' said MacGregor again before going on with the questions.

Mrs Hall answered them all. No, she had never met the late Mr Knapper before and, if her audience would forgive her for speaking ill of the dead, she was jolly glad to be spared the possibility of ever meeting him again. Luckily no-one could accuse Mrs Hall of being a snob, but there was no getting away from the fact that Knapper was a very nasty little pleb.

'Absolutely no breeding, you know. In fact, if he'd been a goat,' declared Mrs Hall roundly, 'I'd have had him parcelled up and in the deep freeze before you could say Tropic of Capricorn. There are some strains one doesn't wish to perpetuate.'

'I suppose,' murmured MacGregor, 'that you get all sorts interested in stamp collecting.'

Mrs Hall's mouth twisted sourly. 'Most of 'em are pretty decent,' she allowed. 'I just didn't happen to take to Knapper.'

Since Knapper was not her type, Mrs Hall doubted if she'd so much as passed the time of day with him during the whole weekend. She was unable to tell MacGregor if Knapper had chummed up with anybody else much because, frankly, she'd had better things to do with her time than go mounting a round-the-clock watch on that jumped-up, snivelling little Yid.

'Yid?'

For the first and only time, Mrs Hall looked taken aback. She bit her lip and muttered something about well, she wouldn't be surprised. Then she pulled herself together and belted the ball back into MacGregor's court by expressing the hope that the interrogation was now at an end. 'Mavis and I ought really to be getting back. We're up to our necks in goats at the moment.'

But MacGregor hadn't finished.

No, said Mrs Hall with evident impatience, there had been no quarrels of any sort between anybody as far as she knew. The group only existed thanks to their shared interest and it would be a sad reflection on philatelists in general if a few of them couldn't spend a weekend together without squabbling.

And no, she couldn't recall whether she had left the Holiday Ranch on the Sunday morning before Mr Knapper or after. Probably before. 'I didn't hang around. As soon as I'd had breakfast and done my bit of packing, I was off. Far too much to do back here, don't you know.'

82

'We had to get that stuff off for Packets for Our Own Poor hadn't we, dear?' chirped up Mavis from her seat by the door. She turned to MacGregor, anxious that Mrs Hall's philanthropy should not go unnoticed. 'She'd collected such an enormous parcel of old clothes, you wouldn't believe! I offered to help her bundle them all up but – oh, no! – she had to do it all herself. That's her all over,' concluded Mavis proudly. 'Insists on seeing every job through from start to finish.'

'Oh, do shut up, Mavis!' It was no doubt humility which made Mrs Hall's voice so sharp. 'I don't think that that was when I sent the POOP bundles off, anyhow.'

'Oh, yes, it was, dear!'

Mrs Hall rode roughshod over the contradiction. 'I do so much charity work,' she told MacGregor loudly, 'that it's difficult to keep track. Always collecting for something. I can't remember why it was I had to come rushing back that weekend and' – she fixed Mavis with an icy glare – 'neither can she!'

MacGregor kindly poured oil by saying that such extraneous details were of little interest to the police, and his kindness was reciprocated by an offer of refreshment. Dover came winging back to full consciousness but even he jibbed at homemade chicory wine and parsnip biscuits.

'I can't bloody well understand it,' he complained later when they'd been conveyed back past the baby goat and through the geese. 'Fancy not having tea or coffee! It's unnatural. They wouldn't,' he added grimly, 'go around eating all that health-food muck if they had my stomach. Chicory wine? 'Strewth, I'd have had the runs for a week!'

'Very odd, sir,' agreed MacGregor. 'Especially when they were expecting us.'

'Eh?'

They had reached the car which was waiting for them out in the lane and MacGregor moved forward to open the door. 'Didn't you notice, sir? Mrs Hall knew all about us – our names, who we were, why we'd come, everything – without us having said a word.'

"Course I noticed!' snarled Dover, in whose gullet the ready lie never stuck. 'Think I'm an idiot or something?'

There was no answer to this so MacGregor covered the hiatus by retrieving Dover's bowler hat from the gutter where it had landed during the complicated manoeuvres required to get its owner stuffed into the back seat. 'Didn't it strike you as odd, sir?' asked MacGregor as he wondered whether he could clean the fresh mud off the bowler without actually touching the patina underneath with his bare hands. 'I didn't phone up to say we were coming.'

Dover had got himself settled and the rear off-side springs protested audibly as they took the strain. He grabbed his bowler hat from MacGregor and clapped it back on his head. 'It was that poncy little toe-doctor!' he growled. 'I'll lay you odds he started ringing round the whole bloody bunch of 'em as soon as we left.' He dropped the blame fairly and squarely where it belonged – on somebody else's shoulders. 'You should have thought of that, laddie, and stopped him.'

MacGregor squeezed into the few square inches of space that Dover had left for him. 'But don't you see how suspicious this is, sir? If that group of stamp collectors are as innocent as they claim of Knapper's murder, why does Pettitt have to tip everybody off that we're on our way? What have they got to hide? We're only making routine enquiries. I think somebody's got a guilty conscience somewhere.'

Dover was paying more attention to the warning rumbles that were coming from his stomach than to what MacGregor was saying, but contradicting his sergeant was a way of life. 'Guilty conscience, my foot!' he jeered. 'It's a simple act of friendship. 'Strewth, if I knew one of my mates was going to have the bloody cops sicked on him, I'd give him a ring and tip him off. Any man with a spark of decency in him would.'

MacGregor was fascinated by this peep into Dover's ethical standards. He hadn't known that the old fool possessed any friends, certainly not any that he would go to so much trouble for.

But Dover's bird brain was already alighting on a more con-

84

crete problem. Like food. 'We're not going to sit here all bloody day, are we?' he enquired. 'I want my lunch. I haven't had a bite since breakfast.' He settled back – a sullen, ungainly lump – in his corner. 'Tell that bloody girl to get her skates on!'

Nine

To his surprise, MacGregor had managed to borrow a car and driver from the police force upon whose patch they were temporarily operating. He naturally attributed this success to his own personal charm as provincial coppers were traditionally disobliging where peripatetic members of the Metropolitan Police were concerned. In acutal fact, the superintendent of the local traffic division had an axe of his own to grind.

He had recently, and unbeknown to his lady wife, taken a rather fetching young policewoman called Elvira under his wing. Elvira, it must be confessed, needed all the help and patronage she could get, as far as her professional duties were concerned. The superintendent had managed to get her transferred to where he could keep an avuncular eye on her but, after one or two hairy experiences, he had grown reluctant to have her driving about on her own. He was, therefore, continually on the look-out for nice little jobs which were within the range of her capabilities and which provided her with a strong masculine shoulder to lean on in case things went wrong again. He wasn't completely blind, of course, to the dangers to which a young girl could be exposed, alone with some randy policeman in a car Elvira herself had probably forgotten to fill up with petrol. This was why, when MacGregor's hesitant request for transport came through, the superintendent had been delighted to help. Chauffeuring a couple of sober and respectable detectives from London round the country was just about Elvira's mark, and she was the 'bloody girl' to whom Dover had been referring.

So far she'd done very well. The roads were quiet, the pedestrians had been keeping their eyes skinned, and McGregor had been doing the map reading. Elvira had driven the two miles from the railway station to Mrs Hall's cottage with practically no trouble at all. But now a sterner task lay ahead – a task, moreover, in which a pretty face and a smashing figure would do her no good at all as Dover was long since past all that sort of thing.

As Dover pictured it, the future was beautiful in its simplicity. En route to the home of Mr Keith Osmond, the next member of the Dockwra Society on their list, a stop would be made at some convenient hostelry for a luncheon break which Dover saw as stretching from opening time to closing time, at least. He left it to Elvira to find the type of establishment he had in mind.

Elvira wasn't entirely to blame for what happened and it wouldn't have made any difference even if she had been able to tell her right from her left.

With MacGregor's help, she set off in the right sort of direction for the small town in which Mr Osmond lived but the route lay across moorland of astonishing bleakness and desolation. If there were any public houses in the vicinity Elvira managed to avoid finding even one of them until well after closing time. She couldn't find top gear, either, but that's another story.

Inside the police car, tempers began to get frayed, tears began to flow and Dover's language became such as would have melted the wax in a drill sergeant's ears. In the end, however, even he had to accept the inevitable and with the illest of ill grace he told MacGregor to tell the stupid little bitch that he'd settle for a snack bar.

Elvira's response to such generosity was to throw back her head and blubber.

Dover couldn't believe it. 'Wadderyemean?' he howled. 'Early bloody closing?'

Elvira took both hands off the wheel while she blew her nose. Lover boy back in Police Headquarters was going to get a piece of her mind about all this! Early closing, she explained damply, meant that everywhere closed early. She might have said more if she hadn't found MacGregor swarming all over her in an attempt to get at the steering wheel before the whole kit and caboodle of them finished up in the ditch.

Dover rose above these petty considerations and, this attack on his personal comfort sharpening up his ideas, grimly spelt it out for Little Miss Dumb-bell: sustenance or else. 'When,' he said, 'we get to wherever it is . . .'

'Gattersby, sir,' said MacGregor, reluctantly surrendering the steering wheel to Elvira. 'It's probably early closing there, too.'

'There'll be somewhere open,' growled Dover. 'And this damn-fool girl'd better find it. Teach her to be a bit more considerate about other people's feelings.'

'There might be a shop,' agreed Elvira, pouting reproachfully at a telegraph pole which had only just missed her front bumper.

'A couple of pork pies,' – Dover had got his requirements off pat – 'a cheese-and-pickle sandwich, a ham sandwich, and one of those apple tart things in a cardboard box.' His face relaxed almost into a smile as he listed the toothsome goodies.

Elvira wasn't used to this kind of thing. 'I haven't got any money.' Well, gentlemen were supposed to pay for girls, weren't they?

'MacGregor'll give you some. Just get cracking, girlie! Drop us off at this chap's place and then, soon as you get back, bring all the grub straight in to me. No hanging about!' He made a nauseating play for Elvira's sympathy. 'It's my stomach, you see. Miss a meal and I'm writhing around on the bloody floor in agony, spewing my guts up.'

Although MacGregor had taken a chance with Mrs Hall and trusted that she would be home when they called, he didn't push his luck too far. He telephoned through and made absolutely sure that Mr Osmond would be at home to receive them. Since Mr Osmond was a salesman for a company marketing bar accessories for pubs and clubs, his working hours were fairly flexible and he agreed to suspend his efforts to boost the sales of personalised beer mats in order to assist the police in their enquiries. Actually, the telephone conversation hadn't been quite as gentlemanly as this summary might suggest, and MacGregor was a little apprehensive about how the interview might develop. Dover didn't care for smart-alec yobboes who couldn't keep a civil tongue in their heads and, unless they really *were* seven-stone weaklings, usually expected his sergeant to do something rugged about it.

Mr Osmond lived in a bed-sitter in a part of Gattersby which was at least handy for the railway station. It was an insalubrious, sullen sort of area and Elvira was quite relieved that she didn't have to wait around out there in the car. There are some things against which even a policewoman's uniform is of little protection.

Dover and MacGregor mounted the stairs to the second floor with that slow-paced dignity which is so typical of our guardians of the law and so appropriate to an unhealthy slob of Dover's weight and years.

Osmond didn't hurry himself about answering their knock and he also took his time about examining their credentials before letting them across the threshold of his room. MacGregor had always thought that commercial travellers were gregarious, open-hearted chaps, ever ready with the quip and the smile. If they were, Osmond must have been an exception. He didn't even look the part. He was a big, raw-boned, heavily muscular young man in his late twenties, with a battered face, a thick neck and large powerful hands. At least MacGregor didn't have to worry about Dover's reactions. Mr Keith Osmond was far too rough and tough a character for the chief inspector to get stroppy with, preferring as he did to restrict his own personal violence to pregnant women, old-age pensioners and small children too young to go telling tales to their parents.

With unaccustomed self-effacement, Dover pussy-footed it across to the chair by the gas fire and sat there, quiet as a mouse.

Mr Osmond resumed his seat at the table, where apparently he'd been writing up his order book, and, tipping his chair well back, propped his feet up on the window sill. Then he slowly unwrapped a piece of chewing gum and slid it into the trap of his strong white teeth. If his behaviour patterns owed much to the stereotype tough guys he'd seen on the telly and in the cinema, it didn't make the air of mindless menace which emanated from him any less disconcerting.

MacGregor resolved to adopt Dover's low-profile approach. Cautiously and carefully he got his notebook out. Somehow one just didn't care to risk any sudden movements in Mr Osmond's vicinity.

'Well, get a move on, darling!' invited Mr Osmond, rotating his chewing gum into the other cheek and scratching himself very unpleasantly under the arm pit. 'Don't be shy!' And then, as though he hadn't got enough stuffed in his mouth already, he helped himself to a cigarette from the packet on the table and lit it with a lighter which threw a flame six inches long.

Dover stared longingly but said nothing.

Trying to treat Mr Osmond as though he were a rational human being, MacGregor began once again to ask the same old questions. How long had Mr Osmond been a member of the Dockwra Society. Had he attended their meeting at Bowerville-by-the-sea? How well did he know Mr Arthur Knapper? Had there been anything about Mr Knapper's behaviour that weekend which had seemed unusual? Had there been any quarrels? Did anybody appear to be harbouring a grudge against Mr Knapper? How had Mr Osmond travelled to the Rankin Holiday Ranch? Had he left on the Sunday before or after Mr Knapper? Well, could he perhaps remember when was the last time he'd actually seen Mr Knapper?

Those answers which were not monosyllabic were obscene. A great deal of Mr Osmond's conversation was decorated with grace-notes of crude, four-letter bawdy and MacGregor was soon thinking of how nice it would be to take a piece of lead pipe and wrap it round the young punk's ears.

Mr Osmond got out a large sheath knife and began casually to manicure his fingernails with it.

The interview was getting nowhere.

Mr Osmond knew nothing about anything, or if he did he wasn't talking.

MacGregor glanced at Dover to see if he was ready to call it a day. He was. Even if it meant getting up out of a comfortable chair and leaving a nice warm room to stand on the pavement outside, Dover was ready to make the sacrifice. He'd had a bellyful of Mr Osmond.

It was at this precise moment that Elvira chose to reappear, pattering triumphantly into the room without knocking and all but getting a fatal dose of cold steel through her throat as a result. Mr Osmond's reactions were razor sharp.

When the dust had settled and both Mr Osmond and Elvira had recovered something of their cool, Dover got his hands on the large brown paper-bag which she'd brought. The girl had done him proud! That brown paper-bag contained a life-support system that would keep even Dover going for the next two hours.

'That's two pounds thirty-five you owe me, sergeant,' said Elvira. She saw that she had caught MacGregor where it hurts. 'You've no idea how expensive things are these days,' she added, opening her big blue eyes very, very wide. She turned away to deal with Dover who was trying to fight his way into a plastic bag. 'Shall I open that for you, chief inspector?' she cooed, and picked up the sheath knife which had fallen from Mr Osmond's nerveless fingers when he'd finally realised that Elvira's entrance did not presage the start of the Third World War or whatever onslaught it was he was expecting.

While she was at it, Elvira unwrapped Dover's sandwiches for him and unboxed his gooseberry and apple tart. She knew how much gentlemen, especially high-ranking policemen, appreciate these little attentions. When she'd finished she returned the sheath knife to Mr Osmond and, for the first time, looked properly at him.

92

Elvira was a very uninhibited girl. Her screams of delighted recognition split the air. 'Well, fancy seeing you here!'

Osmond's response was quieter and less rapturous. 'Bloody hell!'

'Don't you remember me?' demanded Elvira, all poutingly sexy and provocative.

Osmond stood up. 'Oh, sure,' he muttered, looking decidedly less massive and menacing. 'Sure. Once seen, never forgotten, eh? Look – I'll be in touch. Later. Right? Meantime,' – he glanced round at Dover and MacGregor – 'you'll have to take your picnic somewhere else. I'm – er – I'm expecting a visitor.'

Dover warmed to the uncertainty in Osmond's voice and settled back even more comfortably in his chair. Only dynamite would move him now. 'Plenty of room for everybody!' he quipped, waving his ham sandwich to illustrate his point.

Osmonds's face blackened. 'It's private.'

'Good thing I'm broad-minded, then!'

'I've got to go out,' said Osmond, floundering from one patent lie to another. 'An urgent appointment. I've just remembered.'

The Rock of Gibraltar had nothing on Dover. 'You carry on, laddie!' he advised, delicately licking his fingers clean before sinking them in the next sandwich. 'We'll lock up for you. After all,' – the witticisms were flowing like treacle now – 'you can trust us. We're coppers.'

But Osmond was recovering his poise. He reached for his coat. 'All right,' he said. 'Just drop the catch on the door.'

Dover was thick all right, but he wasn't as thick as that. Besides, he felt he owed Osmond something – like a smack across the teeth with a pick-axe handle. 'Hold your horses, laddie!' he snapped and jerked his head at MacGregor.

Correctly interpreting, for once in his life, one of the Master's twitches, MacGregor moved across and cut off Osmond's escape route.

'We haven't finished our little chat yet, have we?' asked Dover with a grin.

Elvira seized what appeared to her like an opportunity to go back and listen to pop music on the car radio. 'Oh, haven't you finished your conference yet? I'm so sorry. I wouldn't have come barging in if I'd known.'

'Conference?' asked Dover who was really firing on all four cylinders.

'Or whatever,' said Elvira with a deprecating little giggle. She adjusted the strap of her handbag on her shoulder. 'I thought you were supposed to be questioning a suspect or something. Silly me! I'm always getting things wrong.'

'We *are* questioning a bloody suspect,' rumbled Dover, glowering balefully at Osmond. 'This joker'll be lucky if he doesn't finish up with his bloody toes dangling six inches off the ground.'

'Oh, you are awful!' protested Elvira in a scream of delight.

Fortunately, MacGregor's ears had also picked up the vague nuances which had been disturbing Dover and he was prepared to do something about them, otherwise they might all have been standing around there yet. 'Where did you meet Mr Osmond?' he asked.

Elvira pondered. 'Oh, it was Breadbury Hall, wasn't it? One of those dreadful weekend courses on Race Relations or something that they make you go on. It must have been last year sometime. Actually' – Elvira smiled in happy reminiscence – 'it was quite fun, really .' She turned to Osmond. 'Do you remember that dreadful sergeant we used to call Reggie the Rapist? And that girl from the Lancashire Constabulary who kept taking her clothes off? Ooh, and the things that used to go on in the Visual Aids room after supper! I just daren't tell you, I daren't, really!'

MacGregor denied himself the pleasure of cajoling further revelations from Elvira. 'Do you mean to say that you met Osmond, here, on a course? On a *police* course?'

Elvira blinked prettily. 'What else?'

'For *policemen*?'

'And us girls, too.'

MacGregor swung back disbelievingly to Osmond. 'You mean you're a copper?'

Osmond's face twisted in a grimace of disgust, anger and exasperation. His response, when he managed to force the words out through a rigid jaw, was directed at the fair Elvira. 'You bloody, stupid, god-damn interfering cow!' he snarled and, as if by magic, a gun appeared in his hand.

Ten

'OK!' said Osmond, a trifle more breathlessly than he might have wished. 'OK. Now, let's cool it, shall we? Everybody just stay nice and quiet and then nobody'll get hurt. Right?'

Dover, MacGregor and Elvira gawped goggle-eyed.

'That's more like it!' said Osmond, pathetically grateful when he saw that nobody was about to play the hero. 'Good! I'm glad you're going to be sensible. Now,' – he took a deep breath to steady himself – 'I'm just going to make a phone call. Right?' He backed off towards the telephone. His next manoeuvre caused some anxiety amongst his audience as he tried to dial *and* keep his revolver trained on them at the same time. That nobody got shot probably owes much to the fact that Osmond had forgotten to slip the safety catch off.

The first fumbling attempt at dialling resulted only in the unmistakable tone of the engaged signal.

'Oh, bugger!' moaned Osmond.

Dover reckoned that this could go on for ever and, very gingerly, raised one hand in the air like an incontinent schoolboy wanting to leave the room. For one blush-making moment, MacGregor thought this was precisely what the chief inspector had in mind, but he was wrong. Dover was merely seeking permission to go on with his lunch.

This comparatively innocuous request seemed to arouse the beast in Osmond. 'You move one bloody muscle,' he threatened in a voice verging uncomfortably on the hysterical, 'and I'll let you have it right between the eyes!' He gulped and, after glaring fiercely at his victims, began dialling again.

This time his efforts were successful and eventually the burr-burr was replaced by a faint, interrogative and high-pitched squawk.

'I want to speak to Sven,' said Osmond, his eyes flickering everywhere.

Another squawk.

'*Sven*!' repeated Osmond irately. He spelt it.

More squawks.

'Of course I've got it right, you silly bitch! It's the du Maurier code. Why don't you bloody look it up?'

The squawks grew offended.

'I don't give a monkey's whether it's your first effing day on the effing switchboard or not!' screamed Osmond, threatening the telephone with his revolver. 'Put me through to Sven and be bloody quick about it. For God's sake, this is a flash-flash call, you incompetent cow! You know what a flash-flash call is, don't you?'

The telephone gave forth a few more peculiar sounds but eventually Osmond sagged with relief. 'Sven?' he asked. 'This is Trill. Yes, *Trill*! Rabbits my end, by the way. *Rabbits*! You know – *ears*! Yes, that right. Now, listen, my seams are giving way. What? Well, yes of course I'm bloody sure! I wouldn't be ringing otherwise, would I? What?' Osmond listened tensely for several moments and then took another of his deep, nerve-steadying breaths. 'I am perfectly calm, Sven,' he said slowly and deliberately, 'but I need help. No, there's absolutely no way we can paper over the cracks. Or stitch things together again. I'm telling you – it's all gone in one big bang. What? No,' – he laughed contemptuously – 'not them, not in a million years. No, it was some bloody little tart of a policewoman who just happened to remember me from way back. Nobody's fault. Just one of those things.' And then, more defensively, 'Well, I couldn't bloody help it, could I?'

Nobody else in the room, of course, could hear the other end of this conversation no matter how much they strained their ears, but MacGregor was fairly confident that he'd solved the problem. Bull-necked young men, guns, gobbledy-gook telephone calls and generous helpings of code names could only add up to one thing. Glancing across, he managed to catch Dover's eye and generously mouthed the answer: *Special Branch!*

Dover's facial expression remained as vacuous as ever. Either the theatrical profession had been deprived of a luminary when he had opted for a job with a pension, or the old fool hadn't got the message.

Osmond was still talking. 'OK – Rendezvous Three in sixty. Got you! All four of us, including the girl? Right! What? Use their wheels? The police car? You sure? Suppose I'm cynosure? Well, yes, I suppose we could make it look as though I'm being taken in for questioning or something, but what about your end? No,' – he reached across and raised the edge of the lace curtain – 'it's just a big black car. Hasn't got "POLICE" written on it or anything. OK, you're the boss. See you.'

Osmond put the phone down. 'Come on,' he said, 'we're going for a ride!'

Dover, neither blessed with MacGregor's perspicacity nor enlightened by it, caught his breath. In this atmosphere of violence, firearms and mysterious telephone calls, 'going for a ride' could have a very alarming connotation. However, he didn't allow his natural anxiety to unman him completely. 'I'll bring my lunch with me,' he said, gathering up the bits and pieces.

Prompted no doubt by some recollection of where the talents of Elvira did and did not lie, Osmond made MacGregor drive, and for this everybody was grateful.

'I'll tell you which way,' said Osmond as they piled into the car, 'and no funny business. I've got my gun right here. One false move and the chief inspector here'll get it.'

MacGregor magnanimously put the temptation right behind him but Dover, who was sharing the back seat with Osmond, was highly indignant.

"Strewth,' he protested, 'you're supposed to threaten to shoot the bloody girl first!'

MacGregor was beginning to get bored with all this play-acting. 'Why on earth should I try anything?' he asked. 'We're both on the same side, aren't we? Frankly, I think your whole attitude is rather silly.'

Osmond squirmed. 'You can't be too careful.'

'Rubbish!' said MacGregor.

'It's all right for you,' retorted Osmond. 'I'm the one who's going to finish up dead if anything goes wrong.'

'And you seriously think that Detective Chief Inspector Dover and I are going to put your life in jeopardy?'

'There's the girl,' muttered Osmond sulkily. 'She's blown my cover once.'

MacGregor was unsympathetic. 'If you hadn't lost your head,' he pointed out, 'you could have dealt with that problem without all this fuss. All that's happened now is that you've given her a full-scale mystery to get her teeth into.'

'My boss'll fix her,' said Osmond grimly. 'And maybe I did go a bit over the top when she came barging in, but I've been under a hell of a lot of strain recently. We're not made of iron, you know.'

This plea for understanding didn't soften MacGregor's heart. He reckoned that any young copper who hadn't gone through his baptism of fire as Dover's assistant didn't know the half of it. Let 'em try trailing around with Scotland Yard's most unwanted man and see how they liked it! Good grief, MacGregor could tell stories that would bring tears to the eyes of the most case-hardened coppers. Stories of degradation, humiliation, frustration, consternation, embarrassment . . .

Gradually, and in spite of everybody's individual preoccupations, the atmosphere in the police car grew lighter. MacGregor grumbled himself into a better mood and Elvira was really enjoying just sitting there and looking out of the window without having all those pedals and gears and switches and things to worry about. Dover, of course, was as contented as a pig in muck. He'd polished off the remnants of his lunch and was now about to treat himself to a well-earned nap. Sagging back like a half-filled sack of King Edwards, he gave a belch of pure contentment and closed his eyes.

After a few miles, Osmond leaned forward and spoke softly so as not to disturb Dover. 'How did you come to identify Knapper so quickly?' he asked. 'I mean, one minute the papers are full of a badly disfigured, unidentified body and the next bloody minute there you lot are, waving your truncheons and kicking old Pettitt's door in.' He chuckled. 'God, you put the wind up him, all right! He'll be wetting his pants for weeks! Mrs Hall, now, – well, she's a different kettle of fish. Takes more than a couple of rough-necked coppers to ruffle *her* feathers.'

MacGregor glanced severely at Osmond's image in the rear mirror. 'We didn't even try,' he said stiffly. 'We're only making preliminary enquiries. There's no point in leaning on anybody at this stage.'

Osmond snorted sceptically. 'Now pull the other one!' he invited. 'I'm not one of the mugs out there, you know. You don't have to tell me what happens when a bunch of cops go round asking a few routine questions. Bloody murder! And you toffs from the Murder Squad are no better than anybody else. You go around putting the fear of God into folks for kicks like the rest of us.'

MacGregor maintained a prim silence.

'Anyhow,' – Osmond seemed unaware that his observations might have caused offence – 'you still haven't told me how you got onto it being Knapper so quick.'

MacGregor couldn't see that the revelation of a few minor details about the identification of a murder victim could do much harm. It might even do some good by constituting a favour which one day would have to be repaid. 'We were lucky,' he admitted. 'It seems that shortly before he died Knapper managed to swallow one of those little plastic, blue bead things they use instead of cash at the Rankin's Holiday Ranches.'

Osmond nodded. 'The Funny Money? I remember. God, the

101

chap who thought up that racket deserves a medal! And a ten-year stretch on the Moor! Blimey, I reckon we were paying at least double for a pint of beer. Still . . .' He remembered that it was the tax-payer who was picking up the bill and stopped feeling quite so aggrieved. 'So, old Knapper managed to swallow a bead, did he? Well, well, he must have had more gumption than I gave him credit for. And more imagination. But,' – he frowned thoughtfully at the back of MacGregor's head – 'there must have been millions of people with access to those beads at one time or another. You can't have had time to process everybody.'

'Actually, there aren't as many as you might think,' said MacGregor, continuing to drive along smoothly and steadily. 'The Funny Money patterns are changed every season and each Holiday Ranch has its own individual set.'

Osmond nodded. 'To stop counterfeiting? Yes, I did wonder myself if it might be worth trying to make your own.'

'In those circumstances it didn't take us long to narrow things down to Bowerville-by-the-sea. Even then, we might have had quite a job on our hands if it hadn't been for the venison.'

'Oh, that venison! I'd forgotten that. Saturday lunch, wasn't it? I suppose it's not something they dish up very often.'

'Only for that one particular meal, as it happens. Fortunately for us. Once we'd got that far, it wasn't too difficult to home in on this Dockwra Society.'

'And that led you straight to our charismatic leader, Mr Pettitt, and he pointed the finger at Knapper?'

'Well, Knapper more or less picked himself. Even with a rather unhelpful photograph of the corpse, it was pretty clear which one of you it was. Then we got in touch with Mrs Knapper and she clinched the identification.'

'Easy when you know how, eh?' Osmond leaned forward until his mouth was only an inch or so from MacGregor's ear. 'And then you decided your murderer must be a member of the Dockwra Society as well?'

'The evidence does appear to be pointing in that direction,' agreed MacGregor cautiously. 'Of course, we're keeping an open mind.'

'Of course.'

MacGregor felt it was his turn to ask a question. 'Did Pettitt ring you up and warn you that we were coming?'

'I'd have had his guts for garters if he hadn't.'

'And Mrs Hall, too?'

'She guessed I was probably the next on your list and gave me a tinkle to let me know what I was in for.' Osmond refrained from further comment and, sitting back, slipped a hand into an inside pocket. 'Do you smoke, sarge?'

'Not while I'm driving, thanks.'

'You can give me one!'

Dover, showering dandruff like a bride showers confetti, came out of his catnap as though summoned by the Last Trump. His dictum – that there's some good in everybody – had once again proved correct. Even this sadistic, trigger-happy, stinking young punk had got cigarettes to hand round. And what nice big fat ones!

Dover's greedy fingers inadvertently fumbled not one but two cigarettes out of the proffered packet, but he had a solution for every social solecism. With an easy grin he stuck the extra fag behind his ear. 'I'll keep that for later!' he quipped.

It is not everybody who would contemplate with equanimity the prospect of placing something in his mouth which had been behind Dover's ear, but Dover wasn't quite so fussy.

Osmond could find no response to all this and had to content himself with getting out his lighter and flipping it as close as he dared under Dover's nose.

Nothing happened.

Dover sniggered.

Osmond flicked the lighter again. Sparks flew and the wick seemed to singe a little, but that was all.

'Damn!' said Osmond. 'I was just going to fill it when you two arrived,' he explained, making excuses like a naughty schoolboy. 'That's the trouble with this model. Mechanically they're very simple and they're totally reliable, but they do use a hell of a lot of petrol.'

Dover chalked this up as one to himself and appealed to the rest of the company. 'Anybody got a bloody match?'

The afternoon was already drawing in when they finally arrived at their destination. MacGregor judged that they were at a spot roughly equidistant from Osmond's bed-sitter in one direction and London in the other. For all Dover knew, on the other hand, they might have landed on the moon – and Elvira's bump of location wasn't much better. However, even this unobservant duo did realise that the car had been halted in the darkest and most remote corner of an enormous car park.

On the distant horizon a huge rectangular slab of a building hunched upwards into the sky, many of its multitude of windows already glowing bright against the encroaching gloom. Osmond marched them towards this Mecca at a spanking pace which did little to endear him further to Dover. Elvira had removed her cap and covered up her uniform with a civilian raincoat. She now looked as normal and unobtrusive as any other girl blessed with long blonde hair, a 39:21:38 figure, and a wiggle.

Dover, with MacGregor in frustrated attendance, dropped further and further behind on this long march across the ruts and puddles and boulders of the car park. 'Where the hell are we?' he demanded as he picked his way fretfully round one of the bigger potholes.

MacGregor gave him his best guess on that subject.

'But what's this dump?' Dover flapped an exhausted hand at the twenty-storey building which, true to the nature of its kind, was getting no bloody nearer.

The building was adorned with a simply colossal illuminated sign which, in the circumstances, MacGregor felt he could do no better than read out to his lord and master. 'It's a Houston Hostelry, sir. One of that new chain of American-style hotels they've been opening up and down the country.'

"Strewth!" said Dover for no particular reason. 'What the hell are we doing here?'

'I suppose this is where we're going to have our meeting with Osmond's boss, sir.'

Dover stopped to have a little rest. 'Who's Osmond?' he asked.

The Houston Hostelries were the latest word in do-it-yourself hotel keeping. The only human being that guests had any contact with was the young lady receptionist who accepted the payments in advance for the rooms, and she didn't encourage the development of any more meaningful relationship. Everything else was pre-packed, obtained from a slot-machine, and sanforised. Still, on the plus side, there was no tipping and the hotel was not ungenerous when it came to providing tea bags, instant coffee, powdered milk and strips of paper for cleaning your shoes with.

Osmond didn't even bother going to the reception desk. Instead, he moved over to a large board on which were displayed letters and messages for the clientele. He found an envelope marked 'Mr Trill' and ripped it open. Written on the inside of the envelope were two numbers. Osmond carefully added seventeen to each number in his head, checked his calculations twice, memorised the results and, only then, tore the envelope into tiny fragments and slipped them into his pocket.

Dover, MacGregor and Elvira watched in awe.

'Follow me!' ordered Osmond crisply and led the way over to the lifts. They were whisked up to the seventh floor where, with only a couple of furtive but penetrating glances over his shoulder, Osmond conducted them down the length of a long corridor and tapped elaborately upon a bedroom door.

It must have been a pre-determined code. The door opened, though whoever opened it was careful to remain out of sight. Osmond stood back so that Elvira could go in first. It wasn't some last vestige of olde-worlde courtesy: it was a trap. As soon as she was across the threshold, the door closed with sinister speed.

Osmond failed to reassure Dover and MacGregor with a self-satisfied nod. 'She'll be de-sensitized separately,' he explained as he moved on to the neighbouring bedroom door.

There was yet another bout of complicated tapping and

Dover, for one, put poor Elvira and her fate right out of his mind while he indulged in a few anxious quivers about his own immediate future. 'Strewth, he thought unhappily as he gazed up and down the long deserted corridor, they could just disappear here without a trace! Nobody knew they were here. Nobody'd seen them come into this blooming hotel and a kid of two could make certain that nobody saw them going out. A couple of cabin trunks – and Bob's your bloody uncle!

When the bedroom door opened, Dover, although naturally dying to take all the weight off his feet, went through with considerable reluctance.

Once again, whoever opened the door took good care to remain out of sight until the three of them – Dover, MacGregor and Osmond – were well inside the room.

'Good afternoon, gentlemen! I am Sven.'

More undulating than walking, the man who had spoken moved away from the door. He was extremely tall, extremely thin and noticeably willowy. Hospitably he stretched out a hand in which every bone seemed twice the normal length.

Osmond quickly made the introductions. 'This is Detective Chief Inspector Dover, sir, and this is Detective Sergeant MacGregor. Both from the Murder Squad, of course.'

'Delighted!' murmured Sven, making sure his smile went right up to and included his eyes. He had spent a long time practising this smile and had now very nearly got it right. 'Do, please, sit down and make yourselves at home. There are drinks on the window sill.' The long, bony hand flapped in the appropriate direction. 'I wonder – would you excuse Trill and myself for a couple of seconds while we have a little whisper together in the corner?'

With Sven and Osmond busy exchanging confidences in the bathroom, Dover started feeling a lot happier. He stretched himself out full length on the bed and watched MacGregor pour out a good stiff whisky. 'Bit of all right this, eh?' he queried amiably. 'Are there any fags in that box? Oh, smashing!' He helped himself to a handful. 'This is what I call pushing the boat out!'

MacGregor was less enamoured of the situation. 'Personally, sir,' he said as he handed Dover his drink, 'I prefer to keep well away from Special Branch. You hear some very funny tales about them.'

'Garn!' scoffed Dover whose pangs of inter-departmental jealousy were soluble in Scotch. 'They don't scare me! They're nothing but a bunch of lily-livered ponces with all this bloody silly cloak-and-dagger stuff. They're not what I call real coppers at all.'

'Perhaps not, sir, but the fact remains that they carry a great deal of weight. What they say goes.'

'Not where I'm concerned it bloody doesn't!' boasted Dover. 'Hey, quick, give us a refill! They're coming back.'

Eleven

'Subversive?' squealed Dover, although Sven obviously hadn't finished speaking. 'You must be joking! All they do is collect bloody postage stamps!'

Sven, now wearing the dark glasses he'd forgotten to put on earlier, remained calm and enigmatic. 'Things are not always what they seem, Chief Inspector.'

'Come off it!' invited Dover. 'I've bloody met 'em! A toe doctor, a potty old woman who breeds goats and What's-his-name – the fellow who got croaked – a piano tuner. If that's all that's threatening the safety of the realm, we can sleep easy at nights. You must have gone barmy!'

Osmond seemed upset. 'The Dockwra Society is just a cover,' he explained earnestly. 'Designed to allow members of the group to maintain contact with each other without arousing suspicion. It's a technique this bunch use a lot. Almost all their cells function under the disguise of specialised clubs of pigeon fanciers or chess players or nature lovers or something. It happens to be an extremely effective way of running a seditious organisation.'

'It doesn't sound effective to me!' sneered Dover. "Strewth, you've apparently infiltrated it easy enough. And you've got 'em so well trained they phone you up and warn you the cops are coming.'

109

Sven leaned forward – a simple movement which seemed to take him ages to accomplish. 'We have indeed managed to penetrate the innermost recesses of this organisation, Chief Inspector,' he murmured, 'but this was by no means easy, not at this level. I doubt if we could do it a second time. Even if we could, it would take years of painstaking effort. That is why my masters' – he smiled deprecatingly – 'we are most anxious – adamant, even – that the cover of young Trill here should not be blown. We are dealing with a matter of national security which must, should there at any stage be a conflict of interests, take precedence over the investigation of a mere murder.'

Dover was now sinking into a rather nasty little hollow which his weight had made in the bed and seemed likely to be buried in the assorted detritus he couldn't help shedding wherever he was. The hollow was gradually but inexorably filling up with cigarette ash, dandruff, fragments of potato crisps, salted peanuts and even the odd trouser button (Mrs Dover being no less fastidious than the rest of us). All in all it was not an edifying sight and Sven might be forgiven for pigeon-holing Dover as an easy pushover. Apart from the evidence of his own eyes, Sven was also fully briefed as to Dover's past career and achievements. The briefing had been somewhat rushed and superficial but the picture which emerged of a man who was stupid, work-shy, prone to gratuitous violence and probably dishonest was reasonably clear. Some of the finer detail was missing, of course, such as the true story of how, by a series of unhappy incidents, Dover had got himself seconded as a supernumary to the Murder Squad in the first place. Nor was there any account of the tireless but unsuccessful efforts every succeeding Murder Squad commander and Assistant Commissioner (Crime) had made to get rid of him nor of the anguish they experienced when they found that there wasn't anybody in the entire Metropolitan Police Force who would have him.

What no curriculum vitae could have been expected to reveal, however, and what Sven failed to appreciate is that, although Dover was a right bastard, he was a lucky one. He was a survivor. They might call him Scotland Yard's most unwanted man. They might complain that he made their posh new head-quarters off Victoria Street look untidy. They might claim he had trouble remembering his own name and that he wouldn't recognise a clue if it jumped and bit him. They might even assert that his usual method of picking out the murderer was by means of a pin, but what they couldn't deny was that Dover was still there. Hundreds of far better men had fallen by the wayside while he plodded shamefully on – determined to draw his pension or bust. Dover had been bloody-minded from the cradle and he was buggered if he was going to change now.

He eyed Sven with dislike. Toffee-nosed git! 'What is it this time?' he demanded. 'Bloody Reds under the bed again?'

Sven and Osmond exchanged knowing glances.

Sven adjusted his sun glasses. 'No, not communists as it happens.'

'The IRA, p'raps?' guessed Dover, winking violently at MacGregor so that he shouldn't miss the exquisite humour of these exchanges. 'Another bunch of thick Micks coming to try and take a rise out of us?'

'It's an extreme Right Wing organisation,' said Sven, slowly unwinding himself and rising to his feet. 'Very extreme. Very determined. Very cunning.'

Dover blinked. 'Do you mean that What's-it-called lot?' he asked curiously. 'You know – that bunch Sir Who's-your-father runs?'

Sven was bouncing about gently on the balls of his feet. He liked to give the impression that he was a man who kept himself physically pretty fit.

MacGregor broke in to try and clarify the situation. 'I think the chief inspector means Sir Bartholomew Grice and the Steel Band mob, sir.'

Sven looked pained at this blatant breach of security. The choice of the hotel room had been completely random and Sven himself had checked for unauthorised bugging devices but, even so, junior detectives from the Murder Squad shouldn't presume.

'The Steel Band organisation,' said Sven loftily, 'is just the tip of the iceberg. What you might call the base of a pyramid whose sharp end is hidden in clouds of deception and fraud.' He hurried on so as not to give anyone time to try and work this out. 'It exists merely as a propaganda exercise, just to let the people of this country know that there *is* a neo-fascist organisation in our midst, and to attract recruits.'

'What you call a "front",' said MacGregor, anxious to show that he had mastered the jargon.

Sven's smile was condescending. 'Quite,' he agreed. 'Now, they vet all their new-comers very carefully and those they consider have real potential are invited to step – as it were – behind the scenes. Only when they've proved themselves reliable and dedicated at this level are they permitted to advance higher, to where the real power and nerve centre of the organisation is located. It can take years and you don't need me to tell you how difficult it is to penetrate a movement as cautious and security conscious as that. The people behind the Steel Band – and behind Sir Bartholomew because he's merely a figure-head – are shrewd and cunning. They make very few mistakes and, when they do slip up, they correct the error with total ruthlessness. That's why we considered it a great feather in our caps when we managed to get young Trill here right inside. It's taken no less than three years of hard and delicate work to do that and you may as well realise here and now that I have no intention of allowing anybody to bugger it up.'

Oh, well, we all have our problems.

Dover certainly did. With a sigh he dumped his whisky glass on the bed-side table and began heaving himself to his feet. Since he gave quite a passable imitation of a stranded whale in its death throes, he caught and held everybody's hushed attention.

'Mind if I just use your toilet?' Being Dover, he couldn't just leave it at that. 'I've got this stomach,' he explained as he waddled at something of a lick across the room. 'Anything upsets or disturbs me when I'm eating, like' – he broke off to glower at Osmond – 'having bloody guns pointed at me, and it

112

gets me right in the guts. Shan't be a sec!' He banged the bathroom door behind him.

It was a long wait. MacGregor drifted off into a lovely daydream about this smashing detective chief superintendent with piercing blue eyes and a lantern jaw and who took such a really keen fatherly interest in . . .

Osmond, who – heaven only knows – had got more than enough urgent problems to be thinking about, was wasting his time in idle and lickerish speculation about the fair Elvira. Gosh, what wouldn't he have given to have been the one detailed to de-brief her . . .

Sven, on the other hand, was staring in pathetic disbelief at the counterpane which still bore the marks (and probably always would) of Dover's presence. There was the mud from his boots at one end and a nauseating mélange of scurf and grease where his head had rested at the other. Sven couldn't repress a shudder. No computer write-out or even a portrait-parlé could prepare one for this sort of thing! And those appalling clothes! The bowler hat that looked as though it had been used for pig swill and the overcoat that any down-and-out worth the name would have jibbed at wearing. Sven simply couldn't understand it. The Murder Squad was reputed to be full of bushy-tailed whizz kids so why on earth had they let this over-weight, ill-mannered lout loose on the poor, unsuspecting public? Sven tried to close his ears to the unspeakable sounds emanating from the bathroom and sought for a silver lining. Well, maybe this Dover slob was actually a better bet than one of the bright boys. He wouldn't be worried about furthering his career or chalking up yet another brilliant success. No, – Sven began to cheer up – Dover would opt for the easy way out every time. He'd be more than happy to soft-pedal the whole Knapper business and let it slide quietly into oblivion.

'Thing is,' grunted Dover as he flopped back on the bed again, 'I still can't fathom why you're getting in such a sweat over the Steel Band. They're just a bunch of nutters, if you ask me.' Dover had slipped into a gregarious, unbuttoned mood –

and MacGregor wondered if he should draw attention to the fact by mentioning it.

Sven naturally didn't agree with Dover's assessment. 'The Steel Band is potentially a very dangerous and subversive element,' he insisted. 'Surely you've read their hand-outs? They want to restore flogging and hanging, reintroduce conscription, send all the blacks back home, expel the Jews, restore censorship, outlaw strikes, abolish trade unions, make homosexual activities of any kind a criminal offence and repeal all legislation dealing with equal rights for women.'

"Strewth,' said Dover, bestirring himself to accept another glass of whisky, 'don't we all?'

'Well, yes,' agreed Sven reluctantly, 'but we don't go shouting the odds about it, do we? Besides, I told you – that sort of thing is just a sugar coating for public consumption. Their real aims are a good bit nastier.'

'Give me a for instance!'

'Well, elimination of the mentally unfit, the abolition of parliamentary democracy, forced labour camps, imprisonment without trial, suspension of habeas corpus and so forth. They're all set to introduce a Nazi style regime into this country with all the additional advantages that modern technology can give them. Good God, man, think what a chap like Hitler could have done with computers and television!'

Dover sniffed and wiped his nose on the back of his hand. This might not have been the most cultured behaviour, but it was a lot more hygienic than using the filthy rag he called his handkerchief. 'And old Sir What's-his-name's going to be the new fuhrer, is he?'

'We think they may have somebody else up their sleeve, actually. Somebody more charismatic and less squeamish than Sir Bartholomew.'

'I don't see,' said Dover, going off into an enormous yawn, 'what' – his dentures clicked audibly back into place – 'all this's got to do with my murder. It's no skin off my nose whether the suspects are a bunch of blackshirts or a gaggle of Girl Guides.'

Sven wasn't the first man to find Dover heavy going. 'That's what I'm trying to explain to you. You see, young Trill here may be able to help, but only on condition that we have your absolute guarantee that in no way and at no time will you place his undercover activities in jeopardy.'

'Ah,' said Dover. Or it might have been a belch.

Sven struggled on. 'We could just deny all knowledge of Knapper's murder,' he pointed out, 'and leave you to get on with it as best you could.'

'Withholding information from the police?' Dover leered happily. 'You'd not know what hit you, mate!'

'We're well aware of our obligations, Chief Inspector, and we want to help if we can. But I must insist first on your total discretion. Trill's position in the inner councils of the Steel Band must be protected and preserved, come what may.'

Dover rolled over onto his back and clasped his hands across his ample paunch. All this talk was boring the bloody pants off him. 'All right,' he said suddenly, 'provided your Little Lord Fauntleroy coughs up the beans, I'll see he's kept out of the limelight.'

It was a capitulation so slick, so total and so artless that MacGregor came out in a cold sweat. Surely even on so short an acquaintance Sven could see that Dover wasn't to be trusted as far as you could throw him?

But Sven, like the rest of us, saw only what he wanted to see. He beamed across at Dover.

'Mind you,' Dover went on, 'all bets are off if he's the one who croaked Knapper. You can't expect me to risk my blooming career to let somebody get away with murder, even if he is a copper.'

If, thought MacGregor sourly, all the people the old fool had allowed to get away with murder were laid end to end they'd stretch to . . .

'Oh, that goes without saying!' laughed Sven, much enjoying Dover's little joke. 'Well, I'm delighted we've been able to reach a mutually beneficial accommodation.' He nodded at Osmond and indicated that a fresh round of drinks wouldn't come amiss. 'Now, there's just one snippet of bureaucratic nonsense to deal with before we hear Trill's story – the Official Secrets Act. It's a frightful bore,' he apologised as he took a couple of sheets of closely printed, buff-coloured paper out of his brief-case, 'but it would keep my masters happy if I could just have a signature. I expect you've both signed the thing a dozen times before . . . Here, do use my pen!'

Dover, who held much the same views about the Official Secrets Act as the Kaiser is reputed to have done about the bit of paper which guaranteed Belgian neutrality, signed without a qualm and nearly got away with Sven's ballpoint into the bargain. MacGregor appended his signature, too, though, since he prided himself on his integrity, there was less excuse for him. He was well aware that he might be faced with a conflict of loyalties in the not too distant future when his obligations as a policeman came up against the needs of state security, but he was in the grip of the eighth deadly sin – burning curiosity. If Osmond had any information bearing on the murder of Arthur Knapper, MacGregor was constitutionally incapable of refusing to hear it.

Sven returned the forms to his brief-case. He felt happier now. Even if these two morons from the Murder Squad did somehow bugger things up, they'd pay for it. Fifteen years apiece he'd get them, especially that fat one.

Sven nodded at Osmond, 'I think you can go ahead now, Trill, old chap, and put your friends here in the picture. Afterwards,' – he directed a toothy smile round the room – 'perhaps they'll reciprocate by telling us how far they've got with their enquiries.'

Dover signified his assent to this proposal with an evil smirk. 'Strewth, what a right gormless long drink of cold water this joker was!

Osmond prefaced his story with an impassioned plea for understanding and restraint. 'You won't forget it's my head on the chopping block, will you? The Steel Band lot don't mess about – and I should know. They . . .'

Dover stirred impatiently on his bed. 'Oh, get on with it!' he snarled.

116

Osmond looked hurt, but he took the hint. 'I joined my local group of the Steel Band as an ordinary member a couple of years ago,' he began. 'I was working under cover, of course, with the object of penetrating the organisation. I naturally don't share their views. Well, these local groups are called Base Battalions and the members really don't do much more than turn up at meetings and rallies and beef up demonstrations and all that sort of thing. They're run by leaders called Base Battalion Chiefs, assisted by a couple of adjutants. There are also several jobs at what you might call NCO level – all with elaborate-sounding titles and distinguishing insignia. Well, I just bided my time. I was keen, but not too keen – if you follow me. Well, before long, I was invited to become what they call a section leader. It was a fairly speedy promotion but not all that unusual. The membership of my Base Battalion was heavily weighted on the elderly and feminine side so any fit young chap like me was bound to be singled out. Well, I just carried on as before. I was conscientious and interested, but not pushy and definitely not nosey. Well, it paid off. One fine day, the Base Battalion Chief sent for me – right out of the blue – and began sounding me out as to whether . . .'

'And,' interrupted Dover, having exhausted the possibilities of loud yawns and the mimed winding up of a watch, 'to cut a bloody long story short . . .'

Osmond flushed. His was, perforce, lonely work and he got little opportunity to talk about it. He'd been quite enjoying having three stalwart colleagues hanging on his every word. 'I was eventually appointed Deputy National Youth Controller,' he muttered sulkily.

Sven moved in to ease the atmosphere. 'Another cigarette, Chief Inspector? And a light? Good! Yes, we were rather bucked with young Trill when we heard the news. Deputy National Youth Controller isn't quite at the hub of the movement, but it's getting there and is not to be sniffed at. Oh, dear me, no! Naturally they investigated him with the utmost thoroughness and we were delighted that his cover story stood up to it all perfectly.'

'Touch wood!' said Osmond, piously patting the plastic top of the built-in dressing table.

But Dover was getting bored. 'All right, laddie,' he growled, 'we've got the picture. You got yourself accepted as a top level, fully paid up, card bearing thug by this bunch of nutters. Congratulations! Now, let's get on to the murder bit!'

Osmond risked a glance of pure hatred at his tormentor and followed it up with a glare at Sven. Well, if your own boss couldn't protect you from fat old fools, who could?

'Did you attend the weekend meeting at Bowerville-by-the-sea in accordance with some sort of instructions?' asked MacGregor, only trying to be helpful and getting a scowl for his pains.

'Yes,' said Osmond. He would like to have limited his answer to this one curt monosyllable, but the temptation to talk was too strong. 'Mr Pettitt sent me an invitation – well, a summons, really – about a week before it was due to take place. Certain code words were used to activate me.'

'Did you know Pettitt?'

'Not personally, no. I knew he was the Southern Regional Leader and Chief Judiciary Officer for the Movement, of course. That put him at least a couple of steps above me in the hierarchy.'

'What about the others at the Holiday Ranch?'

'I'd never met any of them before, and I'm pretty certain they were all strangers to each other as well. I did manage to run their names through the computer, though, before I went to Bowerville. There was nothing particularly remarkable about any of them. They'd all got five or six years' service with the Steel Band, but apart from that they were clean. Except for Mike Ruscoe, that is. He'd got a couple of convictions for drunk and disorderly, but not recently. Oh, and I think Mrs Hall had collected a parking fine in Winchester once.'

'Pettitt sent you the names of the other people who were going to be there?'

Osmond bit his lip. 'Well, no, he didn't, actually.'

'I thought is was a bit unlikely,' said MacGregor, highly gratified to have spotted this. 'So how did you know who to run your computer check on?'

'Well, actually, we've infiltrated Pettitt's chiropody practice,' said Osmond uncomfortably. He carefully avoided catching Sven's eye. 'One of his part-time receptionists, if you must know. She got hold of the list of names for us.'

'Including Knapper's?'

'Of course. There was nothing to single him out in any way at this stage. He was just one of the seven.'

'I see.' Since Dover was now breathing deeply and regularly with his eyes closed and his mouth open, MacGregor felt he could take Osmond through his story at a fairly leisurely pace. 'How did you travel to Bowerville, by the way?'

'By car. As per instructions.'

'And when you arrived?'

'I told them I was a member of the Dockwra Society and I was directed to a bedroom in Hut No. Eleven. Pettitt himself was in the other bedroom in that hut. Well, when we'd all arrived, we had a sort of little get-together in one of the other huts – Number Twelve – when we were all sort of introduced to each other. It was a purely social occasion. We were told that we were to get down to the real business – whatever that might be – on the following morning. That was the Saturday, of course.'

'You met everybody else at this session? Including Knapper?'

'Yes. There was Knapper, Mrs Hall, Braithwaite, the strong-arm laddie called Mike Ruscoe whom I've already mentioned, and another chap called Valentine. Oh, and Pettitt himself, of course.'

'Pettitt was in charge?'

'Yes.'

'And then?'

'Well, we had supper and a few drinks and then went to bed. To be perfectly honest, there wasn't much else to do. Nobody seemed to know what we were there for. Pettitt obviously did, of course, but nobody had the nerve to ask him. They place

119

rather a lot of emphasis on blind obedience in the Steel Band.'

MacGregor nodded. He could well believe it. 'And on the Saturday morning?'

'We all gathered in the common room in Hut Twelve again. Mike Ruscoe and I carried out the routine security checks and then we all settled down to listen to what Pettitt had to say to us.' Osmond paused and, getting his handkerchief out, wiped his forehead and then the palms of his hands. 'It came as something of a bombshell, I can tell you.'

'Oh.'

'He said that there was a traitor in our midst.'

Twelve

Even Dover opened his eyes. He hadn't really been asleep, of course, though that bed was comfortable enough to . . .

MacGregor was nodding understandingly. 'And you thought it was you he was talking about?'

'Not half!' Osmond looked quite sick. 'Talk about time standing still! And then the relief when I cottoned on it was this Knapper fellow they were putting the black on – poor sod.'

'But, in that case, why were you there?'

Osmond looked across at MacGregor in surprise. 'Well, I was part of the court, wasn't I? That's what we'd all been got together for – to try Knapper for betraying the movement.'

'In a bloody holiday camp?' That was Dover making one of his rare but penetrating contributions to the discussion.

Osmond swung round. 'Why not? It was a damned good choice, if you ask me. The place was virtually empty at that time of year and our little collection of huts or chalets or whatever was quite isolated. Nobody came near us the whole weekend because we were on the cheapest rates and so we didn't get any service. We had to make our own beds and, if we wanted any cleaning done, we had to do it ourselves. Meals, of course, we took in the main restaurant which was at least half a mile off. No, I take my hat off to whoever thought that place up. It was brilliant. There weren't even any telephones so Knapper couldn't have phoned for help, even if he'd got the chance. He'd been instructed to travel by train to Bowerville-by-the-sea so that he'd no hope of making a getaway by car and that Holiday Ranch was too far from everywhere to try running for it on foot.'

Dover frowned horribly and snapped his fingers for another cigarette. 'But some of you had cars up there, didn't you?'

'All of us except Knapper, as it happens. But almost the first thing Pettitt did was confiscate all our car keys and hide 'em away somewhere.'

'Interesting,' observed Dover, sinking back and closing his eyes the better to picture the scene. 'Fancy.'

Osmond glanced across at Sven who permitted himself the very faintest shrug of his shoulders. Actually, Sven was just beginning to experience a tiny twinge of doubt. Could all this mowing and moping and general air of seediness be merely a blind? Was Dover, in fact, cleverer than he looked? Well, yes, he'd have to be, if only to keep breathing – but Sven meant *really* clever. Could there perhaps be a brilliant detective lurking beneath that unbelievably sordid exterior? Sven told himself 'no', but he was still plagued with this niggling sense of unease. Had he made a disastrous mistake in letting somebody from the CID get a peep at one of Special Branch's more exotic operations? The CID were always such an envious, vindictive, jealous bunch. As a rule, of course, Sven felt more than capable of running circles round them, but if they were going to produce somebody subtle and devious enough to go around playing the village idiot . . . Sven decided to batten down a few hatches, just in case.

He cleared his throat, caught Osmond's eye and smiled very sweetly. 'I should keep it as short as you can, Trill, old chap,' he suggested casually. 'We don't want to bore everybody with a lot of unnecessary detail.'

A nod is as good as a wink. 'OK,' said Osmond. 'Well, like I said, Pettitt was the boss and he was the one who knew what was going on. His job was to act as president of the court and

122

as prosecutor. He'd been supplied with all the evidence against Knapper. The rest of us formed a sort of jury. Mike Ruscoe – he's a Trooper Colonel in the Special Force – and I were also detailed off to guard Knapper and see he didn't take a powder. We had him handcuffed to a tubular steel chair with two sets of handcuffs. Ruscoe kept one set of keys and I kept the other. That meant Knapper couldn't be released unless we were both there and he just hadn't a hope in hell of overpowering the two of us. Mrs Hall was appointed secretary to the court and was supposed to be keeping a record of the trial, but I don't think she did. Well, it's not the sort of thing you'd put down in writing, not if you'd any bloody sense.'

'Was there a counsel for the defence?' asked MacGregor.

'No, Knapper had to look out for himself. He was allowed to speak and ask questions and make statements on his own behalf but, of course, he'd no chance to call witnesses and no time to prepare a reasoned answer to the charges that were brought against him – up to and including the fact that he was Jewish.'

Dover pried one eyelid open. 'It's beginning to sound like something out of a bloody book!' he charged, unable to think of anything more disparaging than that.

'It was for real all right!' retorted Osmond grimly. 'They were accusing Knapper of infiltrating the Steel Band for the sole purpose of betraying its innermost secrets to some sort of Israeli security agency. Knapper denied it, of course.

'Hey, just a minute!' Dover had been working things out. There were, after all, some subjects upon which he was the acknowledged expert. 'If you'd got this What's-his-name trussed up like a chicken, how did he get over to the dining room for his venison dinner?'

Osmond blinked. 'Well, he didn't. I brought a tray back for him. And for Mike Ruscoe, too. He stayed behind to guard Knapper.' Osmond shivered slightly. 'It beats me how Knapper had the appetite to eat anything, but he did. He downed half a pint of beer, too. Maybe the poor bugger thought we were going to find him innocent or something.'

'But you didn't?' MacGregor was not taking notes. Somehow

he felt that the two Special Branch men would prefer things this way.

'Find him innocent? Not bloody likely!' Osmond's attempt to laugh the question off fell very flat. 'All the so-called evidence against him was just a load of rubbish. Mostly it was just friend Pettitt shouting accusations and abuse at the top of his voice. Mind you, the case for the defence wasn't much better. That was all denials and counter-abuse and counter-accusation. Half the time I couldn't follow what was going on at all, and I don't reckon my fellow judges could, either. Not that it made a monkey's one way or the other. We had to register our verdict by a show of hands. Well, nobody wanted to be standing in Knapper's shoes so, naturally, we all voted with great enthusiasm for guilty.'

Sven felt that some comment might not come amiss at this point. 'It was all most unfortunate,' he explained smoothly, 'but these things happen. It's a question of deciding where the greater good lies. Even if Trill, here, had played the hero and spoken up, it wouldn't have saved Knapper's life, would it? It would merely have cost Trill his, and ruined several years of painstaking and dangerous work into the bargain.'

Nobody seemed to have any response to this and Osmond nervously pulled out another cigarette and borrowed a light from MacGregor. 'Pettitt congratulated us on our verdict,' he went on, exhaling a deep lungful of smoke, 'and then informed us that we had to decide on the sentence as well. Well, we'd no bloody choice, had we? It was treason, and traitors always get the chop. It's an occupational hazard. Well, we thought that was the end of it. Mrs Hall wrote it all out – verdict and sentence – and we signed it. I'm not saying anybody felt particularly happy about it, especially with Knapper blubbering away there and whining and tugging at his handcuffs. Of course, we none of us realised at this stage that we weren't only judge and jury, we were the bloody executioner as well.'

"Strewth!' said Dover. 'You mean Knapper was murdered by a bloody collective?'

'No, I don't!' said Osmond quickly. 'We drew lots for it.'

"Strewth,' said Dover again. He was a man of few words. 'So that means you actually know who . . .'

'It means nothing of the sort!' snapped Osmond irritably. 'If you'd just keep quiet for a minute, I'll explain!'

Now, if there was one thing that Dover was a stickler for, it was proper respect from his subordinates. He appreciated that Osmond was under something of a strain and was prepared to make allowances. Which is why he restricted himself to the promise to come over there and ram the young ponce's snout through to the back of his bloody head should there be any further manifestations of lèse-majesté.

It was Sven who eventually offered the abject apology which Osmond, for some reason, seemed strangely reluctant to make. In due course the previous atmosphere of goodwill and harmony was restored, though both Osmond and Dover had the air of men who were making some quite extensive mental reservations. In Osmond's case these probably didn't amount to much, but Dover prided himself on bearing his grudges untarnished to the grave.

'We drew cards for the job,' said Osmond, taking up his story again in a low, tight voice. 'Well, we were dealt the cards, actually – like a game of bridge. Pettitt produced a brand-new pack and discared all the jokers and the deuces. That left him with a deck of forty-eight cards – eight for each of us. Pettitt included himself in the deal, too, you see.'

MacGregor checked the arithmetic. Pettitt and Osmond made two. Mrs Hall made three. And there were the other men who had not yet been interviewed: Ruscoe, Braithwaite and Valentine. That made a total of six. So, there were six players in this gruesome game and forty-eight cards. That, indeed, meant eight cards each. MacGregor nodded his approval.

One can see why, from time to time, he did tend to get right up Dover's nose.

'We were each allowed to cut and shuffle the pack,' said Osmond. 'To prove it was all fair and above board, I suppose. Then Pettitt dealt the cards. Whoever got the Knave of Clubs was the executioner and thus responsible for putting Knapper

125

to death. Whoever got the King of Spades drew the job of disposing of the body. This was to be done in such a way that a) it would never be found, b) if it was found it would never be identified, and c) if it was found and identified it would never be traced back to the Steel Band and our meeting at the Bowerville-by-the-sea Holiday Ranch. As you will appreciate,' added Osmond with a wry grin, 'the eventual disposal of the body left rather a lot to be desired.'

'Comes of using bloody amateurs,' growled Dover.

'The cards were dealt face downwards on the table in the usual way. When they'd all been dealt, we picked our hands up and looked at what we'd got. Then we chucked them all back, face downwards, in a heap. Pettitt added the deuces and the jokers and we all cut and shuffled them again before they were put back in their box.'

MacGregor pursed his lips. 'That seems safe enough,' he said. 'Only those who got them would know where the two vital cards had been dealt.'

'I'm not so sure.'

'Oh?'

'I reckon Pettitt could have marked those two cards. Pricks on the back or something that he could have felt with his fingertips when he dealt them. After all, it's no great shakes to re-seal a pack of playing cards, is it?'

Dover had been left way behind as usual. 'What's the point?' he asked.

Osmond shrugged his shoulders. 'They'd have a hold on you for life, wouldn't they? They could blackmail you into doing anything for 'em for evermore. Or say you got the Knave of Clubs and just sat tight and didn't kill Knapper. Well, the Steel Band couldn't have let you get away with that, could it? They'd have had to dish out punishment for back-sliding like that – and quick! Me, if I'd been in Pettitt's shoes, I'd have bloody well marked those cards.'

Dover wrinkled up his nose in fierce concentration. 'So that grotty little toe doctor knows who the bloody murderer is?'

'He might,' agreed Osmond, 'but there's no proof. All I'm

telling you is what flashed through my mind – and everybody else's, I'll bet. Whoever got either of those cards must have realised it wasn't only Knapper's life that was on the line – theirs was, too.'

'I suppose there's no chance you were one of the lucky lads?'

Osmond stared with considerable dislike at the grinning Dover. 'My hand hadn't got a face card of any sort in it,' he said loftily. 'And I'd barely had time to grasp that before Pettitt was telling us to throw the cards back into the middle of the table. That meant I didn't get a chance to spot anybody else's reaction.'

'Pity,' sneered Dover. 'Then what?'

'Time was getting on. It was late afternoon and Pettitt obviously wanted to get all his orders issued before supper. He told us that, whoever killed Knapper, they had to strip him as well and put all his belongings in a plastic bag for separate disposal.'

Dover shot into an upright position as though some public-spirited citizen had just sent a thousand volts through him. 'That woman!' He flapped his hands at MacGregor. 'Mrs What's-her-name! The one with the bloody goats!'

'Mrs Hall, sir?'

'A pound to a penny she got rid of the clothes!' Dover sank back exhausted.

MacGregor was not best pleased to have Dover making this connection (however elementary) and in front of witnesses. Dear heavens, another burst of inspiration like this and the Special Branch men would be thinking that Dover was the brains of the partnership. 'Mrs Hall certainly mentioned that she'd despatched a bundle of old clothes to charity, sir. I suppose it's possible that they belonged to Knapper.'

Osmond wasn't interested. 'I don't know how they got rid of Knapper's gear. All I know is the stuff Pettitt told us about how Knapper was to be killed and his body disposed of. Believe me, that was more than enough for me. Pettitt had to tell the lot of us, you see, because nobody knew who the murderer and his mate actually were.'

'You've got to take your hat off to 'em,' said Dover admiringly. 'It's all very clever. Where was Knapper when all this was going on?'

'Right there in the room with us. He heard it all.'

'This Steel Band lot don't mess about, do they?' asked Dover, who would have felt quite honoured to shake the hand of Ghengis Khan. 'I suppose that's when Knapper got the idea of swallowing the blue bead. You were bloody careless there, you know. If it hadn't been for that bead, we'd have never bloody well got started.'

'I know,' agreed Osmond. 'I've been wondering when he managed to do it. It must have been when he went to the toilet. He probably had a blue bead in his pocket or something.'

'Didn't you search him, for God's sake?'

'Only for weapons.' Osmond got to his feet and stretched himself. He was a very physical young man and he was finding all this sitting around in smoke-filled rooms very tedious. He walked over to the window and peered out. 'Who'd have thought a lousy blue bead was going to be that important.'

'Were you told how Knapper was to be killed?' asked MacGregor.

'Lord, yes! Strangled from behind with a piece of cord. Garotting.'

'And getting rid of the body afterwards?' MacGregor was finding it hard to believe all this. Surely even the upper echelons of the Steel Band wouldn't indulge in such sadistic folly? 'Were you given full instructions about that, too?'

Osmond shook his head and resumed his seat. 'No, that was left up to the person concerned. Pettitt said he thought it would be better if the rest of us didn't know where the body was concealed.'

'That's a bit funny, isn't it?' pressed MacGregor. 'I mean, murder's bad enough, but to be suddenly presented with the problem of disposing of a corpse right out of the blue . . .'

'There was plenty of time to work things out,' said Osmond indifferently. 'Several hours. Knapper had to be dead by one o'clock in the morning and the removal of the body was scheduled to start at two, by which time it would have been stripped and the false teeth removed. There was to be a large sheet of plastic to wrap the body in and transport was laid on. I told you all our car keys had been confiscated when we arrived? Well, they were now going to be left out on the table, all labelled with the number and make of the car they belonged to. The "King of Spades" character could use whichever car he wanted to ship the body out in. Yet another way of tying us all in, you see. Even if, like me, you didn't draw either of the vital cards, you could still find yourself in it up to your neck because it was your car that had been used.'

MacGregor stared. 'You were already in it up to your neck,' he pointed out severely.

Osmond flicked a glance across at Sven. 'Well, yes, I suppose so,' he admitted. 'Sort of. Anyhow, I gave my car a damned good clean, inside and out, when I got home. And I'll bet everybody else did the same.'

MacGregor was horrified. 'You might have destroyed some vital evidence!'

Osmond shrugged his shoulders. 'Well, it's done now, sarge. Anyhow, I've told you about all I know. When Pettitt had finished, we all went off and had supper. I brought some food back for Knapper again, but the poor sod seemed to have lost his appetite. Then we all retired to our rooms. Oh, by the way, Mrs Hall moved into Knapper's old room. This meant that the hut where Knapper was being held prisoner had nobody sleeping in it.'

'I shouldn't have thought anybody was bloody sleeping anywhere,' observed Dover, although his own Churchillian ability to cat nap at the drop of a hat was never impaired by anything much, other than a bout of acute indigestion.

'What about this man Ruscoe who was guarding Knapper?' asked MacGregor.

'He stayed on duty till eleven o'clock. Then he went to bed, having first ensured that there was no way Knapper could escape. The killing was to take place between midnight and one a.m. and, when the body had been stripped, the murderer was to return to his own room. Between two and three, the other chap had to come along and do his stuff. Well, say he got back to the Holiday Ranch by seven o'clock – that'd give him something like five hours. Ample time to drive to Muncaster and back – and in winter the gates of the holiday camp are left open all night, and unguarded. It was a piece of cake. When the chap got back, all he had to do was drop the borrowed car keys back in the pile and go to bed.'

'You make it sound very easy,' said MacGregor uncomfortably.

'It was,' said Osmond shortly. 'Proof of the pudding, sarge. I reckon the whole thing went off like clockwork – which is why I can't tell you who killed Knapper and who dumped his body in the rubbish tip. Sorry, but I just don't have the faintest.'

'Stuff that for a lark, laddie!' Dover rose to a half-sitting position in his indignation. 'You're supposed to be a trained detective! You must have spotted something.'

'Well, I didn't.'

'Look, don't mess me about, laddie!'

'I tell you, I didn't see anything.'

Dover's face blackened. 'Try pulling the other one!' he invited threateningly.

'I went to bed and stayed there. With my head under the blankets.'

Dover appealed to Sven. 'Did you hear that? This bloody young whippersnapper of yours claims he went to bed and stayed there while somebody was committing murder not a dozen yards away!'

'I daren't risk blowing my cover,' insisted Osmond. 'Not for somebody like Knapper. Guilty or innocent, he was of no great loss either way. It's a question of priorities. I saw it as my duty to put the welfare of the country as a whole first.'

'Jesus!' exploded Dover. 'Look, we're not talking about being a bloody hero, laddie. Anybody can see you're not the type to go sticking your neck out to save somebody else's life, but you could show a bit of common or garden curiosity, for God's sake! What was to stop you taking a peep through the bloody curtains?'

130

'I had to behave just like any other loyal and devoted member of the Steel Band,' said Osmond, his face pale and his jaw clenched. 'We were told to go to bed and stay there, and that's precisely what I did. That's what everybody did. Bloody hell, we'd just seen what had happened to Knapper! We had a demonstration of what the movement was likely to do to anybody who didn't toe the line.'

'A peep out of the bloody window!' repeated Dover stubbornly.

Osmond gestured irritably. 'You've seen the layout of those huts at the Holiday Ranch,' he said. 'The only window in my room looked straight out across Barbara Castle Prospect to the sea. I couldn't have seen anything in the vicinity of the common room where Knapper was if I'd wanted to. And as for slipping outside – not a hope! I shared a hut with Pettitt, for God's sake! I could hardly risk him, of all people, catching me snooping around, could I? And everybody else was in much the same boat. What with the verandahs and the way the bedroom windows were located and the angle at which the huts were placed – nobody in Shinwell Square could possibly have kept Hut Number Twelve under surveillance. Nobody. Not without going outside in the open. Look, I didn't like the idea of letting a chap get rubbed out like that, but I'd no choice. I had to comply with orders and keep my head down. And, if that's the way I reacted, you can bet your boots everybody else did, too. You've got to understand that they're a bunch of absolutely rabid fanatics. From their point of view, Knapper was a traitor of the worst type and deserved all he was getting.'

Thirteen

Nobody spoke for a long time on the way back. Not that it was exactly quiet inside the police car. Apart from the turned-down chatter coming from the radio, Dover's stomach was rumbling fit to erupt and Elvira was snivelling away to herself on the back seat. Osmond had remained behind at the Houston Hostelry for further consultation with the man who pulled his strings, which was just as well since Elvira had, for the moment, gone right off men and had hysterically refused to share the back seat with even so dead-beat a specimen as Dover. The interview she had had with a couple of Special Branch heavies, not noted for pulling their punches, had thoroughly demoralised her and the threats about what would happen to her if she ever so much as opened her mouth to anybody about anything had so instilled the fear of God into her that it was several days before blazing indignation replaced abject terror. Meanwhile, thanks to her attitude towards men in general and policemen in particular, Dover was sitting in the front of the car.

MacGregor was again doing the driving and really doing it quite well, considering that he had to shift several kilograms of Dover's overhang every time it was necessary to change gear.

'Let's stop somewhere and get a bite to eat,' said Dover after a prolonged bout of highly audible visceral protest. ''Strewth, it wouldn't have hurt 'em to have laid a meal on for us back at that bloomin' hotel.'

MacGregor kept his voice down. 'I think we'd better get rid of the girl first, don't you, sir?'

'Bloody good idea!' approved Dover, generously giving credit where credit was due. 'Look,' – the desire to see the back of old Moaning Minnie sharpened his night vision no end – 'there's a bus stop!'

It was not easy to convince Dover that Elvira could not just be dumped out in the dark in the middle of nowhere nor to persuade him that a bus stop per se by no means implied the prompt arrival of a bus going in the right direction. In the upshot MacGregor simply had to insist that, however inconvenient it might be, Elvira must be delivered safely right to her own front door.

'Bloody women!' grumbled Dover, and screwed another cigarette out of MacGregor by way of compensation.

MacGregor tried to switch the conversation into a less inflammatory channel. 'I'm not at all sure, sir,' he said, 'exactly where we stand at the moment.'

Dover grunted non-committally.

'I mean, are we being expected to refrain from pursuing our enquiries in every direction,' asked MacGregor thoughtfully, 'or have we just got to tread softly in those areas which are sensitive where the Special Branch is concerned?'

'Ah,' said Dover, already at sea.

'Even the latter alternative, sir,' mused MacGregor as he stared blankly ahead through the windscreen, 'is going to present us with a number of problems. Supposing, for example, we eventually identify and charge the guilty person,' – MacGregor was certainly giving his imagination full rein – 'how on earth do we bring him to trial without disclosing motive? And how can we disclose motive without blowing the lid right off this Steel Band business? We can hardly pretend that Knapper was murdered because of some sort of quarrel over postage stamps. But, if we bring the Steel Band into it, how can we keep Osmond out? To say nothing of the fact that he's wide open to being charged as an accessory whatever happens. And' – MacGregor sighed unhappily as the complications piled up – 'what about the Director of Public Prosecutions, sir? Will he accept all these conditions of secrecy and concealment? Are we supposed to keep the true facts from him or are we supposed to tell him but make him sign the Official Secrets Act first?'

'Search me!' grunted Dover. 'Tell you one thing, though,' – he settled back as comfortably as he could in his seat – 'I'm not going to lose any bloody sleep over it.'

Surprise, surprise! thought MacGregor bitterly. 'We shall have to decide what we're going to do, sir.'

'Not tonight, we shan't!' retorted Dover firmly.

'The problem will still be there in the morning, sir.'

'I didn't like the look of that young punk the moment I clapped eyes on him,' growled Dover, going off as was his wont at any old tangent. 'A right cold-blooded fish! Fancy skulking under the bed-clothes while some poor bastard's getting croaked next door!' Dover's indignation might well have been justified. After all, there's absolutely no *proof* that he himself would have slept peacefully through somebody being murdered in the same room with him. He might, or he might not. It would all have depended on how much noise was being made.

'He did find himself in a most desperate situation, sir,' said MacGregor, anxious to be fair.

'I didn't go a bundle on that other chap, either,' said Dover darkly. 'Toffee-nosed, lah-di-dah ponce! Who does he think he is, eh? Laying down the law like a . . .' Since the comparison failed to come tripping easily to the tongue, Dover substituted a contemptuous flap of his hand. 'We don't even know what his proper name is. Or his bloody rank.' Dover's eyes bulged indignantly as a horrible suspicion seeped into his mind. ''Strewth, I'll bet the beggar's junior to me! I'll stake my bloody pension on it! He'll be some lousy, jumped-up detective inspector who's still wetting his bed every night! And he's got the bloody nerve to start pushing me around and interfering with my work. Well, he's got another bloody think coming!' Dover marshalled all his energies for one glorious gesture of defiance which involved the use of only two fingers. 'I don't give a monkey's for him and his bloody bits of paper!' he declared stoutly. 'Nobody's going to stop me doing my duty.'

It was fortunate that MacGregor could recognise hot air when he saw it, otherwise the shock of hearing the chief inspector using four-letter words like 'work' and 'duty' in a non-pejorative sense might have sent him driving the car into the nearest ditch. As it was, he contented himself with issuing the warning he was sure Dover was longing to hear. 'I'm afraid we must take Sven seriously, sir. After all, he has all the power of Special Branch behind him.'

'Bloody Swede!' snarled Dover in what should have been one last token explosion of defiance. But, instead of letting things fizzle gently out in the normal way, Dover lowered his voice. 'Actually, laddie, I've been thinking.'

MacGregor's heart sank. 'Have you, sir?'

Dover glanced over his shoulder to make sure that Elvira's ears weren't flapping. He saw that she was still too cocooned in her own troubles to be bothered eavesdropping on a couple of rotten male chauvinists. 'Punchard!' hissed Dover, revealing his secret weapon with a snicker of triumph.

'Punchard, sir?' repeated MacGregor. 'Our Punchard?'

'Who else?' Dover heaved himself closer to MacGregor and the gear lever disappeared totally from view. Commander Punchard was head of the Murder Squad and Dover's immediate boss. It was not a name, therefore, to be shouted from the housetops. 'Punchard,' hissed Dover, 'and' – his lips approached right up to MacGregor's ear – 'Croft-Fisher!'

'Croft-Fisher, sir?' Even at this moment of extreme tension and high drama, MacGregor couldn't help marvelling how odd it was that Dover could always remember names when he wanted to. 'Commander Croft-Fisher, sir? The head of Special Branch?'

'They loathe each other's guts!' crooned Dover ecstatically. 'Have done for years. Croft-Fisher tried to shoot Punchard once.'

'Oh, I don't think that's quite true, actually, sir.'

''Course it's bloody true!' snarled Dover. 'You calling me a liar? I met a chap who knew somebody who was there when it happened. It was right after Punchard got Croft-Fisher's blue-eyed boy put away for five years for taking bribes. 'Strewth, you'll be telling me next that wasn't a frame-up.'

'Well, actually, sir . . .'

'I know the copper who did it!' yelped Dover. 'He's a bloody chief inspector now. He faked the lot – photographs, tape recordings, bank statements, everything. And planted the marked money in the chap's sofa. You know Punchard – nothing if not thorough.'

MacGregor could see little profit in arguing about these hardy annuals of Scotland Yard mythology. Commander Punchard was a tough, ambitious man and, if he hadn't in reality committed all the crimes of which rumour accused him, it probably wasn't for the want of trying. It was much more important to find out what Dover had in mind – though MacGregor had a horrible sinking feeling that he already knew. 'How do Commander Punchard and Commander Croft-Fisher come into the picture, sir?'

Dover chuckled. 'If you want to go spitting in Special Branch's eye, Punchard's your man,' he said. 'Back you up to the bloody hilt. Through thick and thin. Shoulder to shoulder,' declared Dover, letting his wishful thinking run riot. 'I'm going to see him first thing tomorrow morning.'

'Oh, do you think that's wise, sir?' MacGregor wasn't certain his hands were shaking but he dropped his speed down to twenty miles an hour just in case. Memories of past encounters between Commander Punchard and Dover came flooding in. The wounding aspersions which had been cast, in a bellow penetrating to the furthermost recesses of Scotland Yard, on Dover's work-rate, honesty, intelligence and parentage. The hysterical threats of actual bodily harm if either dyspepsia or constipation cropped up in the discussion again. The awe-inspiring spectacle of Commander Punchard, tears of frustration streaming down his face, kicking his desk to pieces while

Dover went mulishly on trying to squeeze another week's sick leave out of him.

Ah, those were the days.

Not that there'd been anything like that recently. Commander Punchard's doctor had seen to that. Worried about rising blood pressure, apoplexy and cardiac arrest, he had sensibly put Dover in the forbidden-fruit category. Nowadays Commander Punchard kept Dover at a distance, communicating with him only through intermediaries and ensuring that he was assigned to cases as far away as possible from London. Commander Punchard, MacGregor suspected, was not going to be best pleased to see Dover's pasty face and moth-eaten moustache looming up over his mid-morning coffee.

'Only thing to do,' grunted Dover, answering MacGregor's question of three paragraphs back. 'Like I said, with Punchard backing us, Special Branch can stuff it. He won't stand for that bunch of parlour pinks telling us how to do our job.'

'Even Commander Punchard might find himself inhibited by the Official Secrets Act, sir.'

'Garn!' snorted Dover, revealing a hitherto unsuspected veneration for his boss. 'Old Punchie doesn't give that' – Dover achieved a flabby snap of his fingers – 'for all your red tape rubbish!'

Once he realised that nothing was going to stop the chief inspector (except if he forgot or simply over-slept), MacGregor felt obliged to see that protocol was observed. 'Very well, sir,' he said with quiet resignation, 'I'll ring up and make an appointment for you.'

Dover came down from Cloud Nine with a bump. It was three years since he'd actually met the commander face to face and there was clearly no future in giving the pig-headed old bastard prior warning. 'I'll just drop in on the off chance,' said Dover airily. 'No need to make a bloody meal of it. Besides,' he went on crossly as he saw that MacGregor was about to object, 'Special Branch may have a tap on his phones or something. We've got to box this one careful, you know, or we'll be right up the bloody creek without a leg to stand on.'

138

What really happened when Dover finally bulldozed his way into the epicentrum of the Murder Squad has never been revealed. Voices were certainly raised in anger because a complaint was received from as far away as Wellington Barracks, and Dover certainly looked pretty groggy when he came staggering through to the outer office where MacGregor, loyally hoping for the worst, awaited him. There is no proof that actual physical violence was used. Those who claim it was are thought to be relying too literally on Commander Punchard's oft-repeated aphorism to the effect that everybody is capable of murder and, when he saw that effing slob Dover, he knew he bloody well was. Nor is the rumour that Commander Punchard tried to commit suicide anything more than a complete misinterpretation of what happened. Anybody who has ever been closeted in a confined space with Chief Inspector Dover will know that the overpowering desire to get a window open is merely to obtain fresh air and not, usually, to facilitate self immolation.

'You weren't in there very long, sir,' observed MacGregor, who'd made it two and a quarter minutes on his watch.

Dover was still a bit breathless. 'Old Punchard isn't much of a one for messing about.'

They had retired for tea, buns and convalescence to a nearby cafe. Dover was temporarily banned from the canteen in Scotland Yard for trying to consume his lunch while still pushing his tray along the counter and before reaching the cash desk.

'What did he say about our investigation into Knapper's murder, sir?'

'Eh. Oh, that.' Dover reached for a sticky bun. 'Oh, that's OK. Carte blanche. He hardly let me get the words out of my mouth before he was bawling his head off. "Do what you like!" he said. "Just bloody well get on with it!" I like a man who knows his own mind.'

MacGregor poked nervously around his tea cup with one of those plastic spoons that look like a doctor's spatula. 'He understood all the implications, did he, sir? About the interest Special Branch are taking?'

'I though he was going to have a stroke!' chuckled Dover. 'He sort of lifted his fists up to the ceiling as soon as I mentioned Croft-Fisher's name, and shook 'em.'

'But what did he *say*, sir?'

'That Croft-Fisher was a bigger villain than me. And then he told me to bugger off and get on with what I was being paid for, for once in my life. You know what a terrific sense of humour he's got.'

MacGregor abandoned his cup of tea altogether. 'He did understand the position, sir? That we're involved in a case in which Special Branch are intimately concerned and that, if we just go ahead as normal, we may be putting the under-cover activities of one of their men at risk? And that a senior Special Branch officer has specifically and unequivocally warned us off? And made us sign the Official Secrets Act which may expose us to criminal prosecution if we go ahead and do what you tell me Commander Punchard says we're to do?'

Dover wasn't taking too kindly to all this harassment. 'Get out and get on with it,' he said sullenly. 'Those were his very words.'

'And will he protect us if we come into conflict with Special Branch?'

'To the death,' said Dover. 'Action – that's what he wants. Even told me that getting up off your backside was the best cure for piles.'

'You'd time to discuss your health with him, sir?' asked MacGregor weakly.

'Not properly,' said Dover, dampening his forefinger so as to mop up a few remaining crumbs. 'I was too busy talking about my promotion. Do you know what he said when I told him I was overdue for superintendent? He said, "Payment by results!" See what he was getting at? All I have to do is nail this joker who croaked What's-his-name and it's another couple of thou a year in my pocket. At least.' The prospect of such untold wealth made Dover reckless and he despatched MacGregor for more supplies of tea and cakes.

MacGregor didn't find that the likelihood of his being

hanged for a lamb concentrated his mind in the least. Either Dover was erring on the side of wishful thinking or Commander Punchard had gone soft in the head. Probably both. MacGregor picked up the two small brown coins of the realm, which was all he got back for his pound note, and tried to think positively. Would ten years in one of Her Majesty's prisons be any worse than a life sentence of wet-nursing Dover? Not unless he and Dover were called upon to pay their debt to society in the same cell. MacGregor pulled himself together. Whatever happened, Dover would never finish up in jail. If there was one thing the old fool was expert in it was sliding out from under and coming up smelling roses. If there was a price to be paid for tangling with Special Branch, you could bet your boots it wouldn't be Wilfred Dover paying it.

'What are we going to *do*?' echoed Dover in aggrieved tones. ''Strewth, I haven't got over old Punchard yet.'

'It was the commander I was thinking about, actually, sir. You said he was shouting for action. He mightn't be very pleased to find us sitting around doing nothing.'

'Who's sitting around doing nothing?' demanded Dover with a great show of indignation. 'Besides,' – he sank lower in his chair and turned his coat collar up – 'he'll not know we're here.'

'They say he's got spies and informers everywhere, sir,' said MacGregor, knowing you sometimes had to be cruel to be kind, and loving it.

'I'm planning my next bloody moves, aren't I,' whined Dover. 'Why don't you get your bloody notebook out and look busy?'

MacGregor did as he was told. 'Ready, sir!'

'Eh?' Dover glowered. If he thought for one minute that this cheeky young whippersnapper was trying to ... 'Yes, well, we've not finished seeing everybody yet, have we?'

'No, sir. There were still three of the people concerned we haven't yet interviewed.'

Dover was obviously in one of his decisive moods. 'So we'll do 'em!'

'We shall also have to re-interview the ones we've already seen, sir.'

The expectation of such unremitting toil began to leach the starch out of Dover's iron resolve. 'What for?' he asked pathetically.

'We didn't know anything about this kangaroo court when we saw them the first time, sir. We thought we were dealing with a group of stamp collectors.'

'Not me!' boasted Dover, swinging effortlessly into his match-winning mood. 'I never fell for that. I had my suspicions right from the bloody start. I kept telling you what a clumsy bastard that toe doctor was, didn't I? He damned near crippled me. Well, it stands to reason nobody fumbling around in great thick glasses like him could possibly manage with all those fiddly bits of paper. Same thing for that goat woman. She'd be more at home with a pickaxe instead of a pair of tweezers.'

'How about handling a length of rope, sir?'

Dover caught on quickly. 'Too right, laddie! She could have knocked Knapper off as soon as look at him. And so could that sadistic little rat of a toe doctor. He'd a grip like bloody steel. And what about that Special Branch lad? He'd got shoulders on him like a battleship – and he's tough with it. 'Strewth, all three of 'em are more than capable physically of doing the murder or of humping the dead body around afterwards.'

'I don't doubt but that we shall find the next three suspects equally well endowed, sir.'

'How do you make that out?'

'They were hand-picked for the job, weren't they, sir? Whoever selected them knew what they were going to have to do. Naturally, they went for people who could be relied upon to bring in a guilty verdict *and* be capable of carrying out the sentence afterwards. There was no room for even one milksop in that group. They all had to be capable of murder.'

Dover puffed his cheeks out doubtfully. 'Are you including young Who's-your-father in that lot?'

MacGregor was well versed in the way Dover's – for want of a better word – mind worked. 'Osmond, sir? Why not?'

142

Dover sniggered. ''Strewth, I'd like to see their faces if we nicked Osmond, eh? They'd have a bloody fit. It might be worth it, just for a laugh. Old Punchard'd be over the moon.'

'Yes, I expect he would, sir.' MacGregor had more than a touch of prig about him and sometimes it showed. He just didn't see anything funny about arresting an innocent man for murder, even if he was a member of Special Branch. 'Well, shall we be making a move, sir?'

Customers were beginning to come into the cafe for an early lunch and the aromatic smell of beefburgers, tomato sauce and chips made Dover even more reluctant than usual to get up and go. 'Where to?'

'To see Mr Michael Ruscoe, sir. He's expecting us this afternoon. I took the liberty of giving him a ring and arranging a time while you were in the toilet.'

A look of deep disgust spread over Dover's unprepossessing features. 'It's just not safe for a chap to turn his back on you for a bloody instant, is it, laddie?' he asked with studied ambiguity.

Fourteen

A mere thirty-six hours after Dover had set out with such a cheerful heart and light step, however, he came slinking back to London with his tail between his legs. It was, of course, pretty much the story of his life.

At first things had gone well. The train was on time and there was even a buffet car on board which enabled Dover to keep body and soul together for the whole seventy minutes of the journey. When they reached their destination, the promised police car was duly waiting in charge of a driver who may have lacked Elvira's nubile charms but who did, on the other hand, know his right from his left. He conveyed his passengers to Mike Ruscoe's address quickly and safely.

It was probably when Dover clawed his way out of the back seat that life began to turn sour. God knows, Dover knew better than to expect murder suspects to live in palaces, but this was going too far.

'I think it's a sort of garage, actually, sir,' said MacGregor, indicating a battered sign which claimed that the specialities of Mike Ruscoe's body shop were re-spraying and panel beating.

'It's a scrapyard!' insisted Dover as he picked his way through rusting metal and old car seats. 'Any fool can see that!'

The interview was apparently to take place in a tiny wooden office which Mr Ruscoe had constructed from odds and ends in the far corner of his workshop. The accommodation was cramped, but there would have been a sufficiency of room if Dover had not spread himself around so lavishly and if it had not been for the presence of an unexpected fourth party at the meeting.

Dover disliked Mr Ruscoe at sight. He hated all these aggressively body-conscious men who made a fetish of physical fitness and kept rippling their muscles under skimpy tee-shirts. Yes, Dover hated Mr Ruscoe, but it was the intrusive Weemys who really got up his nose.

Mr Weemys was a solicitor, retained by the Steel Band to protect Mike Ruscoe's interests.

Dover could have spat. Indeed, he would have done if he'd been able to draw a deep enough breath in the restricting confines of that smelly little office. Given half a chance he could have run rings round Ruscoe. Not by using his favourite aids to interrogation, of course. Dover preferred to save his fists for expectant mothers, small children and old-age pensioners. Only a moron would contemplate giving Mike Ruscoe a punch up the throat, but it was obvious that the hairy brute was as thick as a couple of planks. Dover could have outwitted him, easy as falling off a log. Given a fair crack of the whip.

But that was just what Mr Weemys was there to prevent. It was soon apparent that the solicitor was one of these pernickety bastards who expect our over-worked and under-paid police force to conduct all their investigations strictly by the book. Even worse, he opened the proceedings by making an admission which took all the wind right out of Dover's sails. The meeting, he announced, of the Bowerville-by-the-sea Seven at Rankin's Holiday Ranch had been convened for the sole purpose of trying Arthur George Knapper for treason.

Dover's chins sagged and even MacGregor blinked in amazement. This knowledge had, after all, been *their* trump card.

It was left to MacGregor to try and regain the initiative while Dover slumped back to his usual slough of indolence. 'Why then was the accommodation booked in the name of the Dockwra Society?'

Mr Weemys could answer questions like that until the c...
came home. He treated MacGregor to a moving sermon on t...
difficult position in which the Steel Band found itself, sur-
rounded as it was by vicious enemies, most of whom were dirty
foreigners and communists. 'These Red subversives are
everywhere,' explained Mr Weemys with a wintry smile, 'and
only too ready to misrepresent us in any way they can. All our
actions and motives are savagely distorted and we have learned
the hard way how maliciously our public image can be tar-
nished. Now, this whole Knapper business was a matter purely
of private and internal discipline. It had nothing to do with
anybody outside the movement at all. It was a scandal, of
course, of the sort which no political party or organisation cares
to have splashed all over the media. We naturally tried to keep
it quiet. That's understandable, isn't it? And reserving accommodation in a holiday camp under an assumed name is not a
criminal offence of any kind. If it were,' – Mr Weemys widened
his death's head smile – 'there would be a marked reduction in
the number of Smiths spending the weekend in Brighton.'

'Are you admitting, sir, that Mr Ruscoe here took part in an
illegal trial at Bowerville-by-the-sea?'

'In an unofficial trial, sergeant, not an illegal one. There is
nothing illegal about the proceedings of a disciplinary com-
mittee. London clubs, trade associations, professional bodies
of all sorts, including the police, have the right to expel unsatisfactory members of their organisations without reference
to any external body whatsoever.'

'They don't have the right to subject them to further punishment, sir, like executing them.'

Mr Weemys stroked the meagre strand of hair which had
been spread carefully across his bald patch. 'Oh, I quite agree,
sergeant, and I'm happy to be able to assure you that no such
punishment was inflicted on Mr Knapper by the ad hoc com-
mittee of which Mr Ruscoe was a member. Mr Ruscoe and his
colleagues simply heard the evidence against Knapper and
listened to his defence. They then considered the facts, decided
that he was guilty of betraying the principles of our movement,

147

expelled him from the Steel Band, as they were empowered do.'

'And that's all, sir?'

'That is all, sergeant.'

MacGregor was having to think very fast. The questioning was reaching a delicate stage and the last thing he wanted was Dover opening his mouth and sticking his foot in it. MacGregor turned to Mike Ruscoe who was perched on the edge of a packing case and looking vicious. 'Was Mr Knapper kept under guard while this "trial" was taking place?'

Mike Ruscoe looked across at Mr Weemys.

Mr Weemys shook his head.

'No,' said Mike Ruscoe.

'What about meals?' asked MacGregor.

'What about 'em?'

MacGregor sighed. 'Did he take all his meals in the public dining room with the rest of you?'

Mike Ruscoe looked across at Mr Weemys.

Mr Weemys nodded his head.

'Yes,' said Mike Ruscoe.

'We have reason to believe that Mr Knapper took lunch on the Saturday in a room in one of the huts while you stood guard over him.'

Mike Ruscoe was lost way back and Mr Weemys took over.

'Reason to believe, sergeant?' he queried with some amusement.

'I'm not at liberty to reveal my sources, sir.'

'Should the matter ever come to court,' said Mr Weemys indifferently, 'you may have to. Meanwhile I should warn you that I will be able to put six witnesses in the box who will swear on oath that Knapper was never at any time kept under guard nor was his liberty of movement impeded in any way whatsoever.'

This spelt out so clearly which way the land lay that even Dover got the message. The Steel Band had produced their story and would stick to it. It might even, thought Dover dejectedly, be bloody true. This would mean that the Special

148

Branch laddie was lying in his teeth but, then, mendacity was second nature to that lot. On the other hand, why should he lie? Dover's brow creased in thought but his little grey cells balked at having to labour without some external assistance. Dover looked up. 'Got a fag, laddie?'

MacGregor shook his head. 'You smoked all mine on the train, sir.'

Dover scowled. There were bloody shops, weren't there? He appealed to Mike Ruscoe.

Mike Ruscoe got very uptight about it. Nicotine spelt certain death to the body beautiful and Mr Ruscoe did not, never had and never would indulge in such a dangerous and dirty habit. It was for Mike Ruscoe something of an oration, especially as he made it without any help from his lawyer.

When his turn came, Mr Weemys managed a deprecating little smile. 'I'm afraid I'm a snuff man, myself.'

All of which left MacGregor with two choices: he could break off the interview and go out and buy some cigarettes, or he could wrap the whole thing up with all possible speed. Taking into consideration that Dover was unlikely to stay sitting on that oil drum much longer, MacGregor plumped for the second option. Besides, this Ruscoe/Weemys combination was raising problems which the two Scotland Yard men really ought to discuss in private without delay.

MacGregor plugged doggedly away in the few moments he calculated he had left. It did no good. The story remained consistent and coherent whether it was Ruscoe or Weemys who provided the answers.

Everything up to the announcement of the verdict at the trial more or less agreed with what Osmond had said. Only the question of whether Knapper had been held in chains and under guard was in dispute. From the verdict on, though, the Ruscoe/Weemys version came down very heavily on the completely innocuous side. Knapper had merely been formally expelled from the Steel Band and, when he left the courtroom, that was the last Mike Ruscoe had seen of him. No, he wasn't claiming that Knapper had left the holiday camp on that Saturday night. He was merely stating that, as far as he could recall, he personally hadn't seen the miscreant again. No doubt it was an entirely appropriate sense of shame that had kept Knapper from imposing his company on his erstwhile companions.

Car keys. Where had Mr Ruscoe's car keys been kept during the weekend at Bowerville-by-the-sea? In his trouser pocket, of course. Or on the bed-side table. Why?

But that was as far as MacGregor dared to go, in spite of Dover's bland assurances that Commander Punchard was ready and willing to back them all the way. MacGregor was afraid to push any harder in case he started arousing suspicions about where the police had got their information from. Once that happened, it wouldn't take a ferret like Weemys long to arrive at Osmond. MacGregor was still very reluctant to blow the Special Branch man's cover but he knew he'd get no more out of Mike Ruscoe unless he took that risk.

Oh, hell!

The decision to bring the proceedings to a close was greeted with universal relief. Dover began waddling back to the police car like a pregnant homing pigeon while Weemys and Ruscoe triumphantly exchanged the Steel Band salute. This consisted in striking the right arm, with the palm rigidly open and facing downwards, across the chest so that the thumb-edge of the hand made contact exactly over the heart. If the description of this simple and sincere gesture sounds complicated, it must be remembered that, where hand and finger signals are concerned, it behoves one to get it absolutely right.

Dover showed unaccustomed vigour in stopping MacGregor joining him in the car. 'You've got some shopping to do, laddie!' he declared, indicating a complete readiness to slam the door shut whether or not MacGregor removed his fingers.

'Shopping, sir?'

'Cigarettes, you fool! And get a couple of packets while you're at it!'

MacGregor turned meekly away and Dover was just about to close the door completely so as to keep out the cold when he found it was being held open by a hand clothed in a warm, woolly glove. It was Mr Weemys.

'I wonder,' said Mr Weemys, baring his teeth in as artificial a smile as Dover's own, 'if I may prevail upon you for a lift?'

'Eh?'

'You are on your way to see Mr Frederick Braithwaite, aren't you?'

'What?'

Many of Mr Weemys's clients were just as slack-mouthed and inarticulate so he wasn't as disconcerted by Dover's pixilated mouthings as he might have been. 'I don't drive myself, you see,' he explained as he bent forward and ducked his head, 'and it would save me taking a taxi. We've all got to do our bit to conserve fossil fuels, haven't we? So kind!'

'Push off!' said Dover as understanding dawned at last. 'Beat it!'

'But we're both going to the same place, Chief Inspector!' objected Mr Weemys, trying to deflect Dover's clenched fist away from his nose.

'Shove off!' snarled Dover.

MacGregor returned in time to catch the tail end of this unedifying little exchange and for a fleeting moment wondered if Mr Weemys was trying to bribe Dover. Then he decided that Mr Weemys wouldn't be such a fool and nor would Dover be repelling such an overture with quite such a display of fury.

'The cheeky beggar was trying to scrounge a lift!' snorted Dover, scrabbling away at the cellophane wrapping on one of the packets. 'I sent him off with a flea in his ear!'

'To Braithwaite's place, sir?'

'Or wherever,' agreed Dover, going quite limp as he dragged the first lungful of smoke down.

'Doesn't it strike you as odd, sir, that the Steel Band suddenly seems to know every move we make?'

'Not especially,' said Dover.

'We arrange to see Ruscoe, and Weemys is there waiting for us. We fix an interview with Braithwaite, and Weemys is going there, too. When we get round to Valentine, I suppose Weemys'll be there as well, holding his hand.'

'Sure to be,' said Dover, happily letting a lump of cigarette ash drop down his waistcoat and take its chance with the gravy, dandruff, soft-boiled egg and beer stains that were already there. 'Natural enough, if you ask me.'

'But they didn't bother laying on this sort of protection when we went to interview Pettitt and Mrs Hall, sir.'

'That's because we didn't know they'd anything to do with the Steel Band, did we?' asked Dover impatiently. 'Now all that side of it's out in the open, they're just taking a few sensible precautions.'

MacGregor shook his head. 'But how did they know we're no longer swallowing that stamp-collecting society story, sir?'

'Search me,' said Dover glumly.

'Somebody must have tipped them off, sir.'

'Well, it wasn't me, laddie!'

'Nor me, sir. And it couldn't have been Pettitt or Mrs Hall because, as far as they were concerned, we knew nothing about the Steel Band connection at all. That only leaves one other possibility.'

Dover sank deep into his overcoat. 'You're not suggesting Special Branch spilt the beans, are you?'

'If they did, sir, they've put a very neat spoke in our wheel. The Steel Band are going to admit to everything except murder. And with the whole bunch of them telling the same story, we're going to be up against a brick wall.'

'Garn,' said Dover without too much conviction. 'Special Branch wouldn't shop us like that. I mean, why should they? What's in it for them?'

'It could be one way of ensuring that Osmond remains the Steel Band's little white-haired boy, sir,' mused MacGregor, trying to pick his way through the confusion. 'You can see how he'd play it. He'd pretend that we'd found out about the involvement of the Steel Band in the Holiday Ranch meeting, and even that we knew there'd been a trial. By warning them, he's given them a chance to concoct a new story. And that's why Weemys has turned up. It's his job to see that they all stick to the authorised version and to make sure that we don't manage to worm any more of the real truth out of them.' MacGregor shook his head in despair. 'The question is – would Special Branch really go to these lengths just to bolster up Osmond's image as the perfect Storm Trooper?'

Dover fished out another cigarette and lit it in a shower of sparks from the stub of the first. 'The leak doesn't have to have come from Special Branch.'

'But there's nobody else, sir.'

'There's Punchard,' said Dover, trying to yawn without taking the cigarette out of his mouth first.

'Commander Punchard, sir?' MacGregor bent down to prevent too big a hole being burnt in the car carpet. 'I don't think he's very likely to be trying to do the Special Branch a good turn, do you?' He pushed the cigarette back between Dover's stubby fingers. 'You said yourself that there's no love lost between him and Commander Croft-Fisher.'

'He wouldn't give Croft-Fisher the dirt from under his fingernails,' agreed Dover sleepily. 'But who said it'd be Special Branch he was trying to help?'

MacGregor pulled back as far as he could so as to get a proper look at Dover. Surely the old fool wasn't suggesting . . ? And with that damned police driver drinking in every word! 'Sir, you don't think Mr Punchard might be . . .'

Dover grinned evilly through another yawn. 'A member of the Steel Band himself, laddie? Why the hell not?'

MacGregor got his handkerchief out and dabbed helplessly at his lips. Why not, indeed?

Fifteen

Thanks to a touch of Dover's old trouble, which involved a lengthy halt at a public convenience, the police car came in a bad second to Mr Weemys's taxi and the lawyer was already comfortably ensconced in Mr Braithwaite's office by the time our two detectives were shown in.

Except for the more luxurious surroundings, the proceedings were irritatingly similar to those in Mike Ruscoe's miserable hovel. Under Mr Weemys's discreet and deferential guidance, Freddie Braithwaite – as he'd been known all those years ago in the Navy – admitted just so much. Yes, indeed, old chap, that smelly little Yid had been found guilty of betraying the Steel Band's most cherished ideals and traditions, and he had been duly expelled from the movement. Good riddance to bad rubbish – what? But – murdered? Good God, no!

'Personally,' said Freddie Braithwaite with an unpleasant chuckle, 'I wouldn't have risked getting my hands infected by touching the miserable runt – and I don't think any of my associates would, either. Besides, mindless violence is simply not the Steel Band's way of doing things. Definitely not our style. On the contrary, it's precisely the sort of thing we're continually campaigning against. You've only got to look at our

155

literature to see that. Remind me to give you a few of our pamphlets before you leave.'

MacGregor looked up from his notebook. The room in which they were sitting – Mr Braithwaite's office – was warm and comfortably furnished. Mr Braithwaite was an architect and, as he was careful to let fall early on, a local government councillor with friends in all the right places. His allegiance to the Steel Band was evident but unstressed. There was a signed photograph of Sir Bartholomew Grice looking statesmanlike, and a small reproduction of the movement's badge in solid silver which was doing duty as a paperweight. Nothing that couldn't have been removed easily, should it prove necessary.

'Are you suggesting, sir,' asked MacGregor, 'that Mr Knapper's death so soon after his mock-trial was just a coincidence?'

'Mr Braithwaite,' Mr Weemys chipped in quickly, 'doesn't have to suggest anything, sergeant. Speculation about the circumstances of Knapper's murder is a matter purely for the police.'

But Mr Braithwaite was wearing his generous hat. 'Oh, I don't mind chancing my arm, Weemys,' he said confidently. 'And, yes, sergeant, I do happen to think that Knapper's demise was a pure coincidence. As far as our disciplinary hearing is concerned, the murder was simply post hoc and not propter hoc, if you follow me.'

Fortunately MacGregor had received a classical education at his very minor public school, and Dover wasn't listening anyhow. The chief inspector, while still trusting that all those bottles on the side table weren't just for show, was giving most of his attention to the tricky task of extracting another of the cigarettes from MacGregor's packet and looking around gormlessly for a light.

MacGregor, conscious of the expensive carpeting and the real leather arm-chairs, started looking around for an ashtray.

Mr Braithwaite produced one – cut glass and the size of a soup plate – and then stared unhappily at the battered cigarette now dangling damply from Dover's bottom lip. Insignificant

156

though it was, it somehow seemed to lower the tone of the whole room. In desperation, Mr Braithwaite picked up the cigar box and offered it to Dover. 'Perhaps you'd care to try one of these, old chap? I don't indulge myself but I'm told they're pretty first class.'

Dover's pallid features broke into the artless smile of an infant glutton who has been told there are two Christmases this year. He reached out with both hands. 'And I'll take one for the wife!' he joshed.

MacGregor, relaxing only when he saw that the cigar cutter was too big for even Dover to think of pocketing, went on with his questions. He eventually managed to think up one or two new ones and began asking Mr Braithwaite about the make, registration number and colour of his car, and also whether he had any connections with Muncaster.

While Mr Braithwaite didn't seem at all bothered by these questions, his new-found friend, Chief Inspector Dover, was most indignant.

'Wadderyewant to know for?' he demanded crossly, removing the big cigar from his mouth so that he could get the words out.

'I intend circulating a description of all the cars involved, sir,' explained MacGregor, hoping to blur over the fact that he'd only just thought of it, 'in case one of them might happen to have been spotted in the vicinity of the Muncaster Municipal Rubbish Dump.'

Dover leered reassuringly at Freddie Braithwaite. 'Not a chance in a million!' he said with a wink. 'Nobody's going to remember anything like that after all this time.'

'And I'm enquiring about prior knowledge of Muncaster, sir,' MacGregor went on, trying to convince himself that all he would get from seizing Dover by the throat would be impetigo in the hands, 'because it's obvious that whoever deposited Mr Knapper's body in the dump must have known it was there.'

'Fooey!' sneered Dover. 'It could have been sheer bloody chance.' He never did have much patience with all these modern, scientific methods of investigation.

'It could, sir,' agreed MacGregor coldly, 'but the Muncaster rubbish tip is off the beaten track, and I doubt if anybody would just come across it by accident.'

'All you have to do is just follow your nose!' tittered Dover who really did love his little joke. 'You could smell that place five miles off!'

MacGregor counted silently up to ten and turned back to Mr Braithwaite. 'Had you ever met any of the other people who took part in this trial before, sir?'

'No, of course not! We were all total strangers to each other. It's always arranged like that.'

'Always, sir?'

Mr Weemys cleared his throat warningly, but Mr Braithwaite was eager to prove that there was nothing to hide. 'Whenever one of these minor problems crops up, sergeant, our movement does everything in its power to ensure that the accused person gets a fair crack of the whip. Inter ·alia, we try to avoid any suspicion of collusion amongst the members of the court. That's why we assemble a complete cross-section – a mixture of sex, age, background, position and function within the Steel Band. In that way, no one element gets any undue weighting. I trust, sergeant,' – Freddie Braithwaite's smile was very confident – 'that that answers your question.'

'Well, it damned well answers mine!' said Dover, fed up with sitting there listening to MacGregor brow-beating an innocent man. It was this sort of going on that gave the police such a bad name! Dover pulled himself to his feet and thus brought the interview to an end which was as unsatisfactory as the rest of it had been.

The sixth and final member of the court which had sat in judgement at Rankin's Holiday Ranch lived so far up north that Dover and MacGregor were obliged to spend the night in an hotel en route. Presumably the ubiquitous Mr Weemys had done the same because there he was, waiting for them when they arrived at Gordon Valentine's house on the following morning. Mr Weemys's manner couldn't have been more hospitable as he welcomed the late arrivals into the lounge.

Gordon Valentine was an assistant bank manager and, since nobody wanted the embarrassment of policemen calling at the bank, he had been granted a couple of hours unpaid leave of absence. The bank manager didn't care for his subordinate's involvement with the Steel Band — extreme political views of whatever stripe were bad for business — and he certainly didn't allow him to indulge in his fantasies during office hours. At home, though, and in his own time, it was a different matter. Even for a couple of hours and for a couple of policemen, Gordon Valentine was defiantly dressed up to kill. He was sporting the full gear — the black knee boots and riding breeches, the iron-grey shirt, the glittering badges, the sinister arm band and the truculent facial expression of your seasoned, battle-forged henchman. It was quite a sight.

Not that Gordon Valentine was really much of a bully boy. A poor physique and thick glasses prevented that. He was also hen-pecked as Dover soon discovered when he attempted to light up his fourth fag of the day.

Mrs Valentine, it transpired, was allergic to tobacco.

Of course, being married to a woman who doesn't allow smoking anywhere in her house, doesn't make a man guilty of murder. But, in Dover's book, it helps.

It was MacGregor who took Valentine through his story. Once again, though, Mr Weemys's briefing had been thorough and every question received an innocuous and succinct answer. Eventually MacGregor broached the question of the blue beads.

Valentine's air of innate superiority remained intact. 'Yes,' he said, 'I bought a couple of quid's worth at the bar. More or less had to. It was the only money they would accept in the Holiday Ranch and there were no pubs or shops nearer than Bowerville. Well, nobody wants to go slogging all that way just for a drink, do they?'

'You're a boozing man, are you?' demanded Dover with all the disapproval of one who has spent many a morning-after thinking about signing the pledge.

'Not specially,' said Valentine, wondering idly if Dover always went about half-shaved. 'I suppose I'm what you might call a social drinker.'

MacGregor stole an anxious glance at his lord and master. Was the old fool on to something?

'So,' growled Dover, looking very fierce, 'you bought a couple of quid's worth of those blue beads to spend on booze, did you?'

'Well, that and other things.' Mr Valentine strongly objected to being classified as a toper, especially when there was more than an evens chance that his lady wife was listening behind the sitting-room door.

'What other things? Fags?'

If this was a trap, Mr Valentine failed signally to fall into it. 'I told you, I don't smoke!' he snapped. 'I might have wanted to buy some chocolate or something.'

'*Chocolate?*' hooted Dover. He leaned forward. 'You a gambling man?'

'Gambling?' bleated Mr Valentine, looking in vain for guidance from Mr Weemys.

Dover looked his victim right in the eye. 'We found some playing cards in that room you tried What's-his-name in. Having a hand or two of bridge, were you? Or poker, p'raps?'

Valentine thought about his answer for a fraction too long. MacGregor wasn't the only one in the room to remember that, according to Osmond, a pack of playing cards had been used to select the murderer of Knapper. 'I don't know anything about that,' Valentine said at last. 'I didn't play cards.'

'Did anybody else?'

Mr Valentine thought carefully about that, too. 'I really don't know.'

Having thus shot his bolt to absolutely no avail, Dover slumped back in his chair and gave himself up to a glassy-eyed contemplation of his boots. MacGregor shouldered the burden of asking the questions once more and eventually brought the confrontation between Mr Valentine and the forces of Law and Order to an end. Nothing as usual had been achieved, unless . . .

MacGregor was still puzzling over what Dover might have been driving at when, several hours later, their train pulled into its London terminus and he was obliged to rouse Scotland Yard's finest from his open-mouthed slumbers and get him out onto the platform. Of course, MacGregor could simply have asked Dover if the question about the playing cards had any deep significance, but even detective sergeants have their pride.

'What a bloody cock-up!' moaned Dover as they sat immobile in the middle of the rush-hour traffic with the meter on their taxi munching up the pound notes like a donkey consuming strawberries. 'Bloody waste of time all round! Old Punchard'll do his nut. We're no nearer to finding out who knocked Knapper off that we were when we started.'

MacGregor forced himself into optimism. 'Oh, I wouldn't quite say that, sir. We've found out quite a lot . . . really. Considering that we started out with an unidentified dead body on a rubbish dump. We've broken through this Dockwra Society business and got through to the Steel Band underneath. We're on the right lines.'

'We still don't know which one of the buggers actually did it,' grumbled Dover. 'I'm all for nabbing the lot of 'em and charging 'em with conspiracy or something. Whichever way you look at it, they're all accessories.'

It was a slap-dash sort of solution and it appalled Mac-Gregor. 'Oh, I doubt if the Director of Public Prosecutions would ever agree to that, sir.'

'In that case we've had it. We'll never thump a confession out of any of that lot. They'll all be a damned sight more scared of the Steel Band bully boys than of me. It'll be that young bleeder from Special Branch all over again – "it wasn't me" and "I was too bloody panic-struck to see anything".'

'You're probably right, sir,' sighed MacGregor, averting his eyes from the ever-clicking taxi-meter. 'If a highly trained copper like Osmond can't tell who the murderer is . . .'

'There's none so blind.'

'Well, we shall just have to keep plugging away, shan't we, sir?'

'Plugging away?' The prospect of yet more unrewarding toil stirred Dover to protest. 'Over my dead body! Look, laddie, it is over, done with, finished. And the answer's a bloody lemon. All we can do now is sit quiet and keep out of old Punchard's way for a bit.'

'We shall have to interview Mr Pettitt and Mrs Hall again, sir. And Mrs Knapper, too. Now we know about the Steel Band implications we shall have to take them all through their stories again. Even they'll be expecting us to do that, sir.'

'It'll be like those three wise monkeys,' said Dover miserably. 'Or worse if that lawyer joker's there.'

The taxi suddenly leapt into life and raced all of a hundred yards in a screaming bottom gear before coming to a halt once more.

'It would,' said Dover when he'd pushed MacGregor off and got himself wedged back in his own corner again, 'be quicker to walk.'

MacGregor seized on the suggestion with pathetic naivety. It just shows how distraught he was. 'Actually, sir,' he said, pointing out Westminster Abbey as a landmark that even Dover might recognise, 'we're only a couple of minutes away from the Yard. We could just nip out here and . . .'

'You know something, laddie?' Dover asked the question with blistering, if weary, sarcasm. 'That sense of humour of yours'll be the bloody death of me.'

In the end, however, they had to reach Scotland Yard and they slipped as unobtrusively as possible through the glass doors. Dover didn't feel really safe, though, until they were actually inside the converted broom cupboard which served them as an office. In a building where space was at a premium, Dover had been allocated a room to himself because they wouldn't have him in the Squad room. BO, as one witty detective put it, has its privileges.

Dover's first action after flopping down behind his desk was to reach out and turn up the radiator. Blood heat was reached in that confined space in a matter of seconds, and half a cigarette later you could barely see across the room. Dover sighed happily. Just time for forty winks before going home.

But, maybe because of the four-hour snooze he'd snatched in the train, sleep eluded him. Naturally he blamed MacGregor.

'Can't you stop rattling that bloody paper?'

'I'm sorry, sir. It's just the pile of stuff that's come in while we've been away. I don't know if you want to have a look at any of it.' MacGregor held up a copy of the *Police Gazette*, but Dover wasn't tempted.

He tried to settle down again. 'Anything on Knapper?' he asked drowsily.

'There's the full post mortem report, sir,' said MacGregor, riffling through several sheets of paper. 'Nothing much that we didn't know already, I'm afraid. Oh, and here's a response at long last from the Central Fingerprint Bureau about Knapper. Goodness, they've taken their time, haven't they? It's ages since we asked them to make a check. Oh well, it only confirms what we'd already deduced, sir. Knapper had no previous criminal record. Ah, that reminds me,' – MacGregor reached for a pencil – 'I'd better get them to run a check on all the rest of that Steel Band bunch.'

'What for?'

'It might be useful to see if any of them have ever been in trouble with the police before, sir.'

'Can't think why.'

Neither, when it came down to it, could MacGregor. 'Do you think I ought not to bother, sir?'

Dover shrugged his shoulders. He didn't object to work in general, of course, only to work in relation to himself. 'Who deduced Knapper had no previous?' he asked fretfully. It distressed him to be unable to knit up his ravell'd sleeve of care.

'Well, we did, sir.'

'Not me, mate!'

'There'd been no attempt to destroy Knapper's fingerprints, sir. Only his face.'

'So?'

MacGregor tried to remind himself that not everbody was blessed with sharp wits and a logical mind. Or even a half-way efficient memory. 'Osmond told us, sir, that whoever got the job of disposing of Knapper's body was supposed to make sure he was unrecognisable as well. That's why the head and face were soaked in petrol and burned.'

'What's that got to do with bloody fingerprints?' demanded Dover. "Strewth, you don't half enjoy stringing things out.'

Fortunately MacGregor was the stuff that martyrs are made of. 'No attempt was made to destroy Knapper's fingerprints, sir.'

'You can't destroy fingerprints by burning the skin off,' said Dover, who got most of his knowledge of forensic medicine off the telly. 'The whorl things go right down to the bone or something.'

'The fingers could have been chopped off easily enough, sir, and disposed of separately from the rest of the body, if there'd been any danger of us tracing Knapper by means of his fingerprints.'

Dover blinked uncertainly. 'Didn't we trace him through his fingerprints?'

MacGregor shook his head. 'No, sir. Don't you remember? We traced Knapper primarily through the blue bead he managed to swallow and the meal of venison he ate. We only confirmed Knapper's identity by comparing the fingerprints on the corpse with those we found in Knapper's house – the ones his wife had missed.'

Dover was frowning. 'I don't remember that.'

MacGregor sighed. 'Well, actually, sir, by the time we got the answer, we already knew beyond a shadow of doubt that the victim was Knapper so I didn't bother troubling you about it.'

'Oh.' For a second Dover wondered if he'd got the energy to have a row about being kept in the picture but, before he'd decided, his mind had flitted off onto something else. 'It doesn't make sense.'

'Sir?'

Dover opened both his eyes – always a sure sign that he was wide awake – and sat up a bit straighter. 'The murderer doesn't bother destroying Knapper's fingerprints because he knows they'll be no help in tracing who Knapper is, right?'

MacGregor weighed his answer carefully. 'I think so, sir.'

'But how did he know?'

'Sir?'

'Use your bloody brains, MacGregor! Look, everybody says that that bunch of nutters who ran Knapper's trial at the Holiday Ranch were all total strangers to each other. Agreed? So – how did the joker who killed Knapper *know* that Knapper hadn't got a police record and that his bloody fingerprints weren't on our files?'

MacGregor just wasn't quick enough.

Dover answered his own question. 'The way I see it, there's only one chappie who could have known for bloody sure that Knapper's fingerprints wouldn't help trace him. One chappie who's already admitted that he got hold of the list of people who were going to be at Bowerville and ran a routine check on them. In fact, when you come right down to it, there's only one bloody joker in that bunch who could have had access to the Yard's criminal records in any case.'

'Osmond,' said MacGregor, hardly able to believe what he was saying.

'Too bloody right!' said Dover. 'Nobody else could have checked that Knapper's fingerprints weren't on file.'

'And nobody else would have been interested in checking, sir,' said MacGregor, getting quite excited as a few pieces of the puzzle began dropping into place. 'Not at that stage. None of them had any idea why they were being summoned to the Holiday Ranch until they got there. They couldn't possibly have known about having to commit a murder and get rid of the body. Osmond didn't know, either, but he was just doing his job as a copper. He probably runs a check on every Steel Band name he gets hold of as a matter of pure routine. So, when the time came, Osmond *knew* he didn't have to bother chopping Knapper's hands off or anything. He knew that, if the body was found, nobody could identify it from the fingerprints. Oh, just a minute, sir!' MacGregor's face fell.

'Pettitt must have known that there was going to be a trial and execution – and that it was important that Knapper's body shouldn't be identified.'

'But Pettitt couldn't possibly have run a check on Knapper through our files,' insisted Dover. 'Besides, he's the one who dealt out the cards, isn't he? Surely to God he wasn't daft enough to deal himself a card that would put his head on the chopper? Then there's the petrol!'

'The petrol, sir?' MacGregor was finding it difficult to keep up. He wasn't used to so much heady animation from Dover.

'The lighter fuel stuff that was poured over Knapper's head and set alight!' yelped Dover, going beserk as he realised he'd solved a case at last. 'Osmond is the only one who smokes! None of the others do.'

'And owns a cigarette lighter that run on petrol!'

'With a flame like a bloody bonfire!' howled Dover. 'And you heard him! He said it used gallons of fuel. I'll lay you a thousand to one he had one of those little cans of petrol stuff with him at Bowerville. It stands to reason. Anybody who smokes as heavily as he does wouldn't risk their lighter running dry on them.'

MacGregor drew a deep, deep breath. 'I think we may possibly be onto something here, sir.'

'I know we bloody well are, laddie! And I'll tell you something else. I'll bet you Osmond's got some connection with Muncaster somewhere. Prior knowledge. That's why he picked the place. You'd better get cracking on that and find out.'

'What are you going to do, sir?'

MacGregor's question was prompted by the unlovely spectacle of Dover trying to hoist his unwieldy bulk into the vertical plane. One of the troubles with their tiny office was that, when one person changed his position, everybody else had to as well. MacGregor found himself being forced into the frenetic quadrille necessary if Dover was to reach the door without shoving the corner of his desk through the window.

'Going to see old Punchard, of course!' explained Dover, puffing hard.

MacGregor had been afraid of that. 'Oh, not so fast, sir,' he begged. 'It's all very speculative so far. In any case, all this business about the fingerprints and the lighter fuel – it's only good enough to tie Osmond in with the hiding of the body. There's not a scrap of evidence to show that he was responsible for the actual murder.

'That's good enough,' said Dover philosophically. He was always more than willing to settle for second best. 'He'd not get a longer sentence for strangling the poor bastard, would he? Besides,' – he made another surge in the direction of the door and trapped MacGregor's leg quite painfully behind the filing cabinet – 'once we charge him with anything, what do you think the rest of 'em are going to do? They'll all gang up on him and swear blind that he got both cards in the deal.'

'Oh, sir!' MacGregor was growing more and more unhappy as he saw the control of the case galloping away from him. 'We can't do that?'

'Why not?' asked Dover in genuine surprise. 'It's our job to get a conviction, isn't it? Besides, I reckon it's probably true. Put yourself in Pettitt's shoes. Would you leave Knapper's execution to chance? I wouldn't. I'd pick the most likely-looking beggar in the group and see he got the job or – like now – both jobs.'

MacGregor would dearly have liked to pause and consider these possibilities but Dover's advance was remorseless. 'I suppose it's possible, sir,' he gasped before he was flattened up against the wall, 'that the Steel Band lot had somehow rumbled Osmond and just set him up. Be a bit ironic, wouldn't it? Using an undercover cop to do their dirty work for them?'

'If there's one thing you could rely on that young ponce, Osmond, for,' declared Dover as he finally actually got hold of the door handle, 'it'd be doing his own grannie in if he thought it would pay him. He'd not bat a bloody eyelid. Well' – Dover threw out his chest proudly – 'I've got him stitched up good and proper. He'll live to regret the day he pulled a gun on me, the ambitious little punk.'

'You do realise, sir, that we have no evidence as yet against Osmond for anything?'

Dover dragged the door open. 'We've got motive,' he said. 'He didn't want his cover blown in the Steel Band. We've got opportunity. Well, he was bloody there when it happened, wasn't he? And we've got . . . 'Strewth, that business of not destroying What's-his-name's bloody fingerprints clinches it. Look, laddie, I've done the hard bit for you. All you've got to do is dot the "i"'s and cross the "t"'s. It's a piece of bloody cake! Anyhow, I'll be in with old Punchard if anybody wants me. After I've been to the toilet.'

Commander Punchard might have been highly delighted to have embarrassed his rivals in Special Branch, but actually charging one of their number with murder was a different kettle of fish. Especially when the murder might be considered as having been committed for England, if indeed it had actually been committed at all. At the very least Osmond and his superiors would claim that the lad had been acting strictly in the line of duty.

Thanks to Dover's typically premature announcement that he had solved the mystery of Knapper's death, Commander Punchard had time to consider the pros and cons of the situation. In the end, after much heart-searching, he came to the conclusion that though revenge may be sweet, knowledge of such highly confidential and damaging information is better than money in the bank.

A compromise was reached and the whole incident was hushed up. The great British public were thus enabled to retain their faith untarnished in the police, the Secret Service, the Monarchy, parliamentary government and anything else that took their fancy. Of course, things didn't just go on as before. Changes had to be made. It was generally agreed, even by Special Branch, that young Osmond's services could not be retained, but he went out to join the Mounties in Canada with some brilliant references and recommendations. Commander Punchard's thirst for vengeance was slaked by the award, after a decent interval, of the OBE and a year's secondment to the Bahamas.

And Dover?

Well, Dover would have preferred to have his mouth stopped with gold but, when they offered him promotion to detective superintendent, he took that instead.